LEAF & ECHO PEAK

JO MARSHALL

Copyright © 2011 Jo Marshall
All rights reserved

ISBN-13: 9781523782529
ISBN-10: 1523782528

"This children's book opens a rich and imaginative forest world full of characters whose adventures create a different perspective on wildlife and their interactions due to natural and human-induced climate change and how each adapt with the change. Illustrations are gorgeous adding vibrant stimulation to mind as the reader follows the many ups and downs of the main characters. Much insight into the dynamics of forest ecosystems is provided in following these clever creatures. The book is imaginative and gives an added bonus with the "Watch Over Wildlife" at the end of the book, further engaging the readers."

Dr. Tim Foresman
Professor and SIBA Chair in Spatial Information
Institute for Future Environments
Science and Engineering Faculty
Queensland University of Technology

"Not only is Leaf & Echo Peak an adventuresome and humorous journey of animals and their Twig friends as they attempt to escape a pending eruption of Echo Peak, it is a look into Northwestern natural history and the dynamics between family and friends. Throughout the story, Jo Marshall reminds us that change is how we find new ways to grow. Twigs and their animal friends learn that with adaption and tenacity, life is resilient."

Abigail Groskopf
Science Education Director
Mount St. Helens Institute
Learn more about the return to life
   at Mount St. Helens at www.mshslc.org

"The adventures of Twigs use fantasy to introduce simple science for 8-12 year olds. Twigs and Seeder and all of the other plants and animals live in a scary place where earthquakes and volcanoes are a natural part of the landscape, much like the northwestern United States. The creatures of the woods have long learned to deal with these ecological disasters. Humans have the same responses—ask the elders, leave, run, and then accept the new reality. That's an important lesson hidden in the fantasy."

Eleanora I. Robbins, PhD
Science Explorers Club

*Twig Stories royalties are shared
with nonprofit organizations
concerned with protection of wildlife,
climate change research,
nature conservancy, and
forest preservation.*

Acknowledgements

My daughter Ali Jo and my son John deserve all my love for helping me bring the Twigs adventures to children everywhere. I owe so much to David Murray for his amusing and spectacular art. My heartfelt thanks goes to Dr. Norrie Robbins with the Science Explorers Club and Abi Groskopf, Science Education Director, Mount St. Helens Institute for their invaluable suggestions, edits and guidance. Dr. Tim Foresman, a leading authority on climate change with the Queensland University of Technology generously offered encouragement, and I will be always grateful for his support.

LEAF & ECHO PEAK

For Meema
who could see the forest for the trees

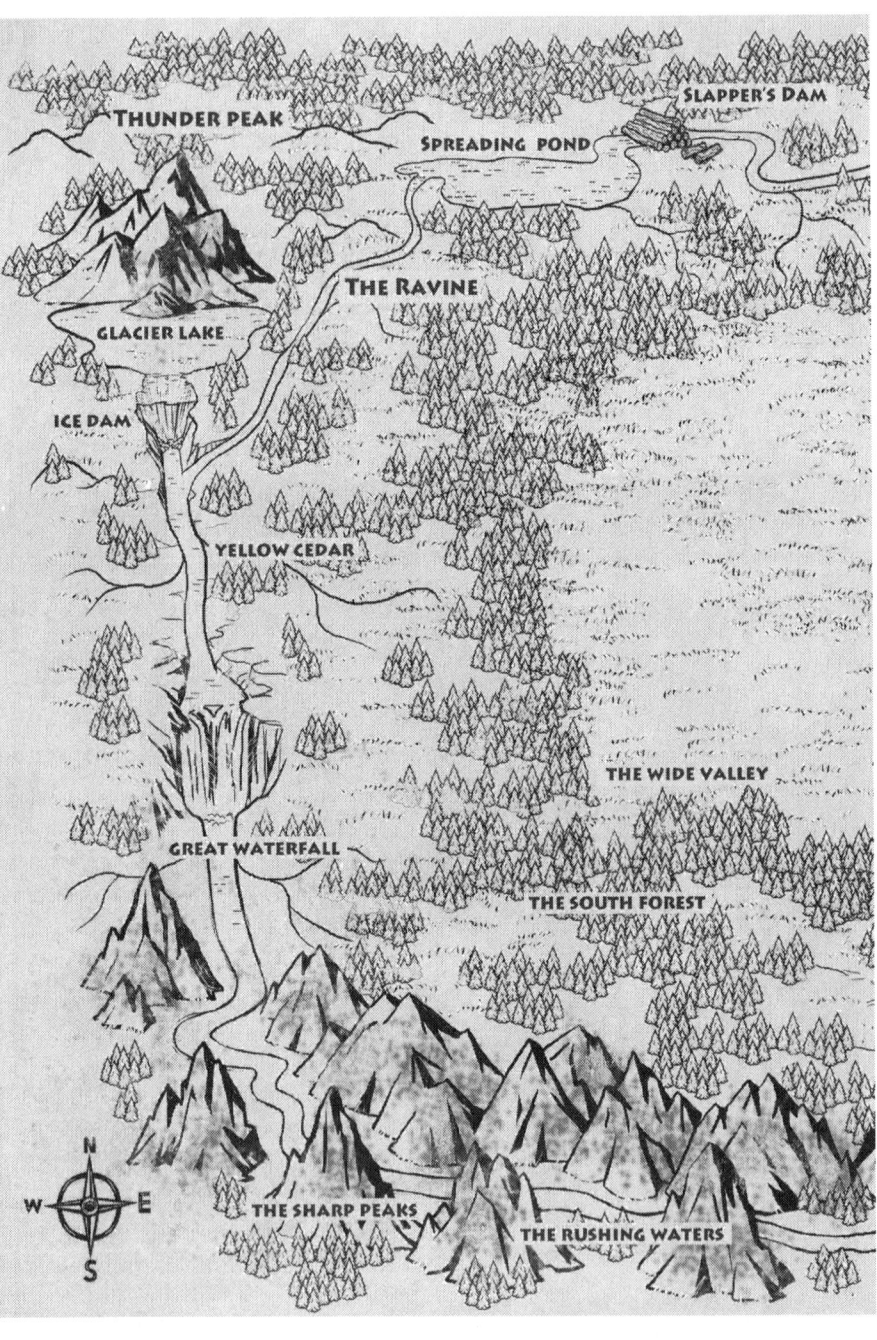

THE NORTH FOREST

THE GORGE

HIGH FALLS

GREAT LOG

THE BLUE MOUNTAINS

THE BLUE BAND

THE WIDE VALLEY

THE FALLS

THE SOUTH FOREST

THE OLD SEEDER

THE SHARP PEAKS

THE RUSHING WATERS

ECHO PEAK

Chapter One

THE OLD SEEDER SHIVERS

Leaf stepped through the knothole door of his haven onto its porch-branch. The limb jutted out halfway up the lofty Old Seeder. He watched a pair of golden eagles soar out of a swirling cloud atop Echo Peak, and float down into the misty Wide Valley. Not far behind, a flock of rosy finches gathered to rest in a nearby grove of aspen trees.

Odd, Leaf thought. *Hookbeaks usually hunt the tiny burrowers on the ice fields of Echo Peak. And roseflutters live on the Long Ice, too, where they eat crawlies blown up high on the wind and scattered across the snow. Why are they here?*

Leaf leaned against the rough, red bark of the cedar. A moment later, faint tremors rippled through the wood. Echo Peak had shifted and rumbled many times in recent days, and cast out trembles such as these from its foothills, but they always faded.

"I wish these annoying land waves would stop," Leaf muttered. *It's been so long since the forest rested. I wonder if the flyers are leaving because of the waves? What else is happening up there?*

Almost against his will Leaf stepped further out on the branch, and searched in the opposite direction from the ancient volcano. Faraway a smoky haze stretched out over the northern horizon and floated above the Great Gorge. Leaf wondered if his Twig friends who lived on its rim had felt the land waves, too.

Mostly Leaf worried about a Twig with gray eyes and silver-white hair. *Is Star safe?*

Compared to the massive sentinel Echo Peak the tallest trees in the forest are mere spindly pines. Except for one tree – an enormous red cedar, which sprouted in the lurking shadow of Echo Peak thousands and thousands of seasons ago. This towering, old cedar dares to grow ever thicker, ever stronger, and ever higher. Dark rings swirl in tight circles around its deep red center, which is its heart. In the Old Seeder's branches all sorts of wild animals flourish, and some not so wild, like Twigs.

Twigs are no taller than starlings, but are often more annoying. There are many Branches of Twigs – the Cappynuts, Sugarpines, Silverleafs, Hemlocks, and many more. One ancient Branch of Twigs sprouted from a red cedar. So they are named the Old Seeder Twigs. Pappo and Mumma, their oldest sprout Leaf, their daughter Fern, and the twins Buddy and Burba live in a large, wandering haven halfway up the mighty cedar tree. The Old Seeder Twigs live so high only the tips of other trees can be seen from their knothole. It is as if an emerald, fluttering sea surrounds them.

Just like past generations of Old Seeder Twigs, they enjoy a cozy haven with convenient knotholes piercing the thick trunk so sunbeams may dance about in the dust. Pappo is always carving another shelf or cupboard somewhere, and Mumma rearranges their robin-eggshell bowls and cappynut cups as each shelf appears. A huge chair stuffed with clumpy moss balls sits in the largest hollow in the haven where they gather to eat and tell stories.

Like all young buds, Buddy and Burba have their own hollow with embroidered feather-fluffed pillows and woven baskets for beds. Fern and Leaf each have their own hollow at the end of long, curving tunnels. Giant, limp leaves hide the tunnels to offer some privacy. Scattered about are piles of colorful leaf-drawings. Fern spends far too much time sketching all the creatures in the forest.

On this morning a bright ray of sun spilled through the open door of the haven, and sparkled in Leaf's emerald green hair. A few strands of leaves hung over his eyes, which were the same color as his hair, for he had not bothered to brush them away. Lost in thought, Leaf tugged at an uncurled bud which had just sprouted from his elbow yesterday. A curious, blue dragonfly with shimmering wings and a long, crinkled body lingered nose to nose with Leaf for a moment, and then flew off to investigate sap dripping in the furrows of the bark.

Pappo and Mumma had left at daybreak to collect willow stems from the muddy banks at the fork of the Blue Band. Willows there made the best baskets. As usual, Leaf, his sister, and the twins were left on their own. Leaf was in charge, although his younger sister Fern and even younger brothers Buddy and Burba knew they were too old now for Leaf to tell them what to do, or what not to do, so for the most part Leaf ignored them.

Bored, Leaf kicked some loose bark from the branch, and watched it tumble down through the limbs to the roots far below. He wondered what he'd do today to pass the time. *Maybe I'll whittle sticks for stabbing things.*

Or carve some forest creatures in the hollow's walls. He yawned and glanced over his shoulder at Fern, Buddy, and Burba who sat in the dust of the haven's floor and twisted dry flax into shapes of beasts. *I should be out hunting in the forest, not stuck here with sprouts.*

"No, twist it this way," instructed Fern. She looped a flax stem over her finger, rolled it off, and grinned. "See? It's a bellycrawler!"

Fern's orange eyes were hidden by limp, golden leaves. This morning, with grim determination, she had fashioned her hair into a bizarre style, somewhat like water spilling over a rock. Fern had journeyed with Mumma and Pappo to the Great Gorge last season. There, she met the brother of Star, a young, white-haired Twig named Moon. Ever since, Fern spent a great deal of time twisting her hair into strange shapes and searching for soft ferns and blossoms to make headbands and decorate her leaf-dresses.

Leaf and Fern first noticed the land waves were growing stronger when the toys trembled and crept across the floor. Then – in a breathtaking moment – the Old Seeder lurched sideways with one massive yank.

"Hang on to something!" Leaf yelled as he grabbed the grizzled face of the knothole.

SCREEEEECH! Panicked birds screamed. Frantic wings darkened the sky. The sound of cracking branches echoed off the granite cliffs of Echo Peak. *CRACK! CRACK! CRACK! CRACK!* It was as if gigantic fists ripped limbs from trees without mercy.

At first Leaf could only hang on to the knothole, and stare with huge, round eyes at the forest below. Then, after one vicious whip of the Old Seeder, he tumbled backwards into the hollow.

"*Ahhhhh!*" screamed Fern. She was tossed upside-down into the puffy chair.

Buddy, and Burba grabbed hold of each other, but were twisted back and forth until they fell apart and skidded across the floor. "*Aaaaaa! Helpppp!*"

Fern turned the color of pale birch as again the Old Seeder lurched sideways. Its massive branches thrashed back and forth as the tree rode the tremendous, rolling quakes.

Buddy shrieked, "Da Old Seeder's shivering!" With arms flailing he slid across the hollow and smashed into a cupboard. At once his fear turned to delight.

"It's shivering! It's shivering!" Burba laughed and shouted as he cartwheeled after his brother.

Buddy shouted, "Da Old Seeder's shivering!" until a cushion smothered his face. Still, his muffled cries could be heard. "Give it my covie!" He pushed his worn, patchwork blankie across the floor toward Leaf. "Give it my covie!"

"It'll stop shivering soon!" Leaf yelled at the buds. He rolled to the door, and caught sight of the forest floor heaving below. His feet flew up in the air and for a moment he walked up the trunk's wall until his toes touched the ceiling, and then he slid back down, tangled up in leafy curtains.

A dust storm billowed up in the hollow. Desperate to keep his little brothers from tumbling out of the open door, Leaf kicked the door shut with his foot. The old tree whipped back in the other direction, and tossed Leaf in the air once more.

Giggling, Burba and Buddy held tight to pillows and somersaulted past Leaf. Buddy's golden eyes twinkled with glee. His hair was a blur of golden leaves. Burba's wicked-looking, orange eyes dared Leaf to grab him as he ducked to avoid his big brother's reach.

Fern tried to grab Buddy as he slid past, but she didn't dare loosen her grip on the mossy chair, so Buddy rolled on by and disappeared into the tunnel, which led to Fern's room.

"Is it a storm?" Fern screamed at Leaf. "Is it the wind?"

Buddy's garbled voice echoed from deep in the tunnel, "Dis is fun! Fun!"

Burba yelled, "Wheeee!"

Eggshell tea bowls fell from the shelves and shattered on the floor. Cappynut cups flew through the air. A stool smashed into Leaf's head.

"Make it stop, Leaf!" Fern howled.

"How do I do that?" Leaf yelled back. His legs flew up from under him, and once more he walked up the wall.

Fern screamed, "Watch out!"

The knothole door wrenched out of its frame and opened with a *WHACK!* Buddy somersaulted from the tunnel straight toward the open door, but Leaf caught his leg just in time.

"It's shivering! It's shivering!" roared Burba.

Outside the trees cracked like lightening, split apart and fell to the ground. The bubbling earthquakes, which had at first only simmered deep in the earth beneath Echo Peak, now heaved the rocks above in a furious boil. They cracked the great slabs of granite and swelled up into gigantic land waves. The South Forest and grasslands of the Wide Valley rode the crest of the tempest, helpless. The earthquakes rolled on and on, violent and relentless, into the foothills of the Blue Mountains far to the east. After a long while the quakes slowed, became soft waves and then ripples until they subsided into the Flatlands in the east and splashed quietly under its prairies. After one last, lingering tremor Echo Peak and the Old Seeder stood silent.

An eerie silence fell over the forest. No birds fluttered. No squirrels chattered. No deer slipped from the shadows to the light.

But two Twig sprouts giggled as they tossed crumpled leaves at each other, and hid behind the shredded curtains in their dust-filled haven.

"Is it over, Leaf?" asked Burba. "Is the Old Seeder gonna shiver again? I hope it shivers again! That was great!"

"Dat's for sure," added Buddy. "Dat was fun! I hope it shivers again!"

Leaf ignored them, and tiptoed to the door. He peeked out through the knothole. Tips of shattered trees slanted in all directions.

Fern peered over Leaf's shoulder, and murmured, "There are no birds, Leaf. What does that mean?"

Buddy and Burba sang, "When's it gonna shiver, shiver, shiver? When's it gonna shiver, eh, eh, eh?" They giggled and threw dusty pillows at each other.

"Hush!" whispered Fern with a frown. "Shhhh! Why don't you pretend to be Hemlock Twigs, and don't talk! Be a Hemlock!"

The buds stared at each other with wicked glee, clapped their hands over their mouths, and tried to smother their giggles. But their slobber burst through their fingers, and became rainbow-hued bubbles, which dribbled off their chins.

Leaf watched a snow-white wisp of smoke curl high into the sapphire-colored sky, and drift away. "Look, Fern. I've never seen a cloud like that before. I think it's floating up from Echo Peak."

"So that means it's all over, right?" whispered Fern. "Echo Peak just needed to burp or something like that, right?"

"I don't think so, Fern," Leaf murmured. "Whatever it is, I don't think it's all over." He watched another white cloud twirl high in the sky, and vanish. "I think it just got started."

Chapter Two

RUSTLE AND FEATHER

Not so far away from where the Old Seeder stood quiet in the chill of the misty dawn, another Twig crouched in a sunny clearing below a jagged, purplish-colored ridge. He peered down into a deep fissure in the earth made by the quake. Granite rubble which had been towering slabs before the quakes now lay in heaps beneath the sheer cliff. Their broken boulders pushed down into the earth like pudgy toes. A nearby creek split apart near the crevice and a thin waterfall fell over the edge. The morning mist drifted atop the crumbling moss, rolled into the crack, and then dropped out of sight. Trees lay uprooted and smashed all around.

"Come look, Feather!" urged Rustle. He leaned far over the edge to take a good look. Beside him clumps of fuzzy moss threatened to fall and disappear into the murky shadows. "It's so deep I can't even see the bottom!"

Being a Twig, Rustle was about as tall as a robin and mostly brown and skinny. But Rustle did not think of himself as small, and he certainly never acted like he was. He had the brash, confident manner of a Twig who had lived alone and survived in the wild for most of his life, which he had. Rustle's eyes sparkled with copper-colored glints. Shimmering leaves, which were the same color as his eyes, sprouted into a mass of long, tangled hair. Rustle usually smirked as if he knew a wicked secret for he believed he knew many whether he really did or not.

Being skillful in the ways of the forest, Rustle draped himself with hunting tools that Twigs needed to survive in the forest. Across his back he had slung a tall walking stick. Twigs called it a saver because it saves them from trouble. He had tied a misty, gold gemstone in its topmost knothole. The gem caught the sun's rays and blasted a hot beam and burned whatever it touched. The gemstone could also light up dark places like caves. His shoulder strap's pockets were stuffed with pebbles and thorns. A loop of flaxen rope encircled his shoulder and fell across his chest. Ever confident, Rusty wore his tools like his bravado, and that lured him into trouble more often than not.

Now Rustle turned to nod at his dearest Twig friend. He held his arms out as wide as possible. "Feather! Come on and look!" he urged. "It's really wide and deep and dark... and scary... *oooooo!*" A twinkle in his eye dared Feather to join him on the edge. Again, Rustle peered into the fissure's depths. "I wonder what's at the bottom. Come on, Feather. You gotta' see it!"

Rustle and Feather had at first been frightened by the violence of the earthquakes. Along with their two chipmunk friends, Speckles and Claws, they had darted into a honeysuckle thicket and hid until the shaking ended. Once all was quiet, Rustle crawled out and poked the ground with his toes to be sure it would remain still.

It was then he had spotted the fissure. Uprooted trees tilted and slanted over it with their leaves still trembling. Rustle pushed a pine cone over the edge, and rolled it into the crevice. He watched in fascination as it spun around and fell into the gloom. A tiny *smack!* floated up as it hit the ground.

Feather tiptoed closer to Rustle. Being a Woodland Twig rather than a Ridge Twig, her stick body moved with the grace of a wind-swept willow. Today Feather had stuck an exceptionally fluffy swan feather into her headband. It dangled over her nose and tickled it. Irritated, she blew the feather into the air. Although Feather was usually as gutsy as Rustle, she was not so eager to approach the collapsing edge. She hesitated and blinked at the destruction around them. Shredded branches littered the forest floor and gravel still slid down the ridge, bouncing and cracking like lightning bolts. It made her nervous.

Alert to the ways of forest creatures, Feather also noticed the birds had not returned to the trees. *Not a good sign*, she thought. Worried, she tugged the leaves of her bronze-colored hair, and tucked its wispy curls under her headband. Her rosy eyes matched the soft glow of her cheeks.

Like Rustle, Feather had survived most of her life on her own. She grew up in the woods far from the Old Seeder across the Wide Valley. When she was very young a horrific firestorm destroyed their tranquil woods. Lightening burst apart a dried-up, old tree, and at once a furious wildfire erupted. There was no escape for Twigs. Feather's beautiful tree-home was lost and none in her family survived except for her.

Rustle had lived in the same woods, too, back then. But he was only a babe and didn't remember the terrifying fire. When the firestorm swept through the woods Rustle's paps had grabbed him from his crib, and scrambled up the tallest tree he could find. From its tip, he threw Rustle into the updrafts of the fire with a desperate hope he would be lifted on the hot air and escape. Like thousands of sparkling ashes Rustle was blown far across the Wide Valley to the Old Seeder's forest. He had been found by Leaf's family, and they believed he must be a Ridge Twig. Rustle survived the fire, but the memories of his Twig family were lost.

During that same devastating wildfire Feather had been rescued by a courageous chipmunk fleeing the fire. He took her with him to a muddy hole in the river bank, and it was there they survived. The chippie became her dearest friend – Speckles. Stranded together without help, they became inseparable. After the fire Feather discovered and saved two other orphaned chipmunks, Claws and Whisper. But no Woodland Twigs could be found, so Feather lived alone until of course, many seasons later, Leaf and Rustle happened to crash nearby on a giant leaf-flyer. It was only then Rustle discovered his true past from Feather.

What if the land waves return? Feather frowned at Rustle's gleeful excitement. *Why did this dark pit open in the forest floor? What's down there?* She hesitated, tapped her chin, and thought about whether or not she should join Rustle at the edge of the crevice.

Suddenly, Speckles chirped a warning. *"TWRRRRRPP!!"*

Feather glanced back over her shoulder. Speckles chittered again as if he were battling a rattlesnake. *"TWRRRRRPP!!"* Afraid to leave the thicket, Speckles hugged his chippie friend Claws. They had squeezed together between two roots so now they looked like one very fat chipmunk instead of two smaller ones.

Claws rolled his eyes in alarm, drooled, and covered his ears, which made sense only to him. He caught sight of an orange paintbrush blossom, and instantly forgot his fear. He pushed Speckles away, skipped over to inspect the flower, and stuffed its petals in his mouth. Then he spotted a worm, yanked it from the dirt, stuffed it in his mouth, and began foraging for more.

Speckles' eyes lit up. He scrambled from the thicket, joined Claws, and stuffed a worm and orange blossoms in his mouth altogether, mashing them for a while with a thoughtful expression.

Feather shook her head and muttered, "I didn't think you were *that* scared." She took a step closer to Rustle, but paused, again. She called back over her shoulder, "Stay away from here now, you two! It's not safe!" She tip-toed to Rustle's side.

Chippies didn't understand Twig words, but it didn't matter anyway. They had discovered a stash of pine nuts left by a gray nutcracker, and now lost all interest in Feather and Rustle.

"Rustle, get back from there!" Feather barked out an order as she tugged his shoulder strap. "Really, you have no sense at all."

"Wait, Feather!" Rustle pushed a clump of moss over the edge. "Listen for how far it falls! Listen for the smack!" Grinning, he rolled another huge clump of dew-soaked moss into the dark.

All of a sudden a tornado of big-eared bats swirled up and out of the crevice! Disturbed when Rustle dropped the clumps of moss into their dark home they whirled in a thick, angry mass. *SHOOSHHSH!* The noise of hundreds of bat wings pounded the air.

"AWWKKKAAK!" Rustle screamed. He covered his head with fistfuls of moss. "Hide!"

"Nightraiders!" Feather shrieked. She yanked out clumps of moss and lay flat beneath them.

WHOOSH! WHOOSH! Disturbed from their roost, and confused by the bright sun the big-eared bats soared out of the ground, and whirled up into the sky in search of a less distressing place to sleep through the day.

"*TWRRRRRPP!!*" shrieked Speckles. The two chippies tried to claw their way under a rock.

At last it was quiet. Feather and Rustle peeked out from under their moss covers. Speckles and Claws returned to scrounging for worms.

"Look what you did, Rustle," Feather accused him. "Stop throwing things in that hole."

Just then, the land waves began again. In the moment it takes a heart to beat, Rustle and Feather felt the earth take a sickening lurch. The ground heaved up and collapsed again and again. A tree near the fissure slid over the edge. The rocks above Rustle and Feather slid down the ridge.

"Hang on!" Rustle shouted. But the moss he'd taken hold of was loose. For a moment he was able to balance at the edge of the pit, but the moss ripped completely out of the dirt. Helpless he reached for Feather just as she reached for him. Their fingertips met as Rustle slipped into the blackness below.

"Rustle!" Feather screamed.

From a distant place far below Rustle's voice drifted up, "Feather..."

Feather turned and yelled at the two chippies, "Speckles! Claws! Find Leaf! Get Leaf!"

Speckles and Claws froze, shocked by Feather's shouts. Orange blossoms and long, green stems dangled from their mouths. They watched as Feather grabbed a thick clump of moss, perched at the edge of the dark pit as if she intended to leap into its depths, and then did.

"Rustle, I'm coming..." Feather's cry faded into the depths.

Speckles blinked. *Strange.... Did she yell Leaf?* Claws lost interest, shrugged, and crammed more pine nuts in his cheeks.

The sun grew warm as the morning passed. Speckles yawned. Claws had already snuggled into a warm hollow in the thicket. He lay with his paws curled against his chest.

For some reason Speckles could not nap. *Did those silly Twigs forget about us? Maybe they fell asleep somewhere.* Speckles felt uneasy. *Feather shouted something to me.* He thought about her shouts. At once he realized, *Feather wants me to find Leaf.* Speckles hopped on top of his sleeping friend, and patted his head in a blur of furious paws.

Claws snored, turned over, and blew an orange petal off his nose.

Speckles snorted with impatience. He chirped a shrill *"TWRRRRRPP!!"* in his friend's ear. Without waiting any longer, he scrambled over a fallen tree, and hastened down a deer path which led toward the Old Seeder.

Claws sat up, and scratched his ear with his foot. With a sigh, he hurried after Speckles.

CHAPTER THREE

NIGHTRAIDERS

Rustle and Feather lay stunned in suffocating blackness. But it was not total blackness. High above, a slender crescent of light shimmered from the split in the earth created by the quake. A thin ribbon of water fell beside them and splashed on the rock floor. Its echoes disappeared into the dark.

"Feather," Rustle whispered, although he didn't know why he was whispering. "Are you alright?" He propped himself up on an elbow and squinted into the murky shadows before and behind him. Prickles crawled up and down his arms.

Feather groaned, "Where are we?"

"Shhh, keep your voice down," Rustle cautioned. He spoke quietly, "I think we're in a cave. It feels like some huge, empty space. Just listen to the water's echoes. I thought I heard scratching…"

They tilted their heads, listened, and blinked at the sliver of light far above. The trickle of water fell and twisted about like a squiggling worm.

"Maybe not a cave," suggested Feather. She rubbed her head and sat up. "The echoes come back to us from both ways. It's more like a tunnel."

"Yes, a tunnel," agreed Rustle. "Listen to how far away the echoes flow. It's a really, really long tunnel. Maybe it runs from here all the way to Echo Peak." He glanced at Feather. The idea sounded ridiculous even to him.

"Well, if it does then that's good," Feather replied. "There must be plenty of ways to get out."

Rustle frowned at her. "Why did you jump in here? You could've been splintered!"

"Well, you're welcome that I came to help you!" Feather retorted.

They scowled at each other until with a flip of her hand Feather looked away. "Anyway, I sent Speckles for help." She smoothed the leaves on her head until they lay flat. She felt to be sure her swan feather was still tucked into her headband and her rock shard was still stuck in her belt. Satisfied, she sat still with her chin in her hands and her elbows dug into her knees.

Rustle jumped up and kicked a rock off the wall. It made a loud *CRACK!* The harsh noise bounced back and forth in the tunnel, and made Rustle and Feather cringe.

"Shhh! Did you say you heard scratching? I bet there are cave creatures here," murmured Feather. "Maybe more nightraiders? Or did they all fly away?"

Rustle walked around in circles peering into the dark. "Lots flew out, but there's probably more." He ran his hand over the smooth, curved walls. "It's so weird. It looks like a tube that a worm makes, don't ya think, eh?"

"Yes, like a giant worm path through the dirt, only this one is through rock... black rock." Feather stood up. Her legs felt shaky. She realized her eyes were becoming accustomed to the murkiness. "I can see better now."

"Me too." Rustle answered. He squinted to see the walls better. "It's like... a *really huge* worm crawled right through this rock! I bet giant worms live here, eh, Feather?"

"Oh, stop it, Rustle. You're not scaring me," Feather snorted. "What would a worm do to us, anyway?"

Rustle shrugged. "It'll eat you!" He turned around and kicked over the clumps of moss he had thrown into the crevice earlier.

"What are you doing?" asked Feather.

"I lost my saver," Rustle grumbled.

"Oh, that's great!" Feather joined the search. She struggled to turn over giant clumps of moss which had fallen into the crack during the quakes.

"Finally!" Rustle tugged his walking stick from under the huge pinecone he'd tossed in earlier.

At that same moment a tiny, gray, rubbery-looking snake slithered right between Rustle's feet. "*AAAAHHH!*" he screamed.

With calm sarcasm Feather asked, "Really, Rustle?" She watched the snake slide away. "You scared it! Just look at the poor thing. It doesn't even have teeth...or a nose... or eyes even. That is pretty weird." Feather laughed. "I guess it has feelings, though. I bet it feels its way around, eh?"

Embarrassed, Rustle stabbed his saver into the back loop of his shoulder strap, and mumbled, "Oh, for moon's sake, come on! Let's find a way out of here. The day's not flowing any slower!"

Feather grinned. "You sound like an Old Seeder Twig, Rustle. Pappo will be happy you remember his old saying – the day's not flowing any slower. And you even said it right. Not like me. I always say, 'the sky's not getting any higher' or 'the toad's not burping any louder', eh?" Her voice softened. "Anyway, do you think Speckles will find Leaf?"

Rustle sneered at the idea of a chippie figuring out anything much less finding their friend Leaf. "Well, even if he can find him it's not like Speckles will tell him what happened to us." At once he regretted what he'd said because Feather looked so dismayed. He took Feather's hand, and patted it. "Don't worry. If any chippie can get a Twig to understand that we need help, Speckles will. Still, I don't think we should wait around here. We better find a way out on our own. I wonder which way to go?"

"Look." Feather pointed south. "The water's spilling that way, so it must be downhill. Do you see anything down there? A bit of light is shining. Maybe we should follow the light, eh?"

Rustle brightened up. "Well, even if it's not a way out I can still catch a little light with my saver and shine it on down the tunnel. Then we can do the same when we reach the next spot of light until we find a way out." He pulled the saver from its back loop, stuck the tip on the rock floor, and twisted it until the gemstone at its top caught a beam of light from above. A bright flash stabbed the dark shadows far down the tunnel.

Feather gasped. "Look at that. The tunnel is so long even the light is lost!" Now she hesitated to leave the spot where they fell. "What if Speckles comes back with Leaf? Shouldn't we wait here? Or try to climb out right here?"

The Twigs looked up, and then at each other.

"Yes, maybe we can climb out here, eh?" Rustle wondered. He ran the light beam over the smooth rock walls. No handholds. No footholds. The walls were sheer and curved over making a climb upwards difficult. "I think we'd fall before we could even start up. "It's like the rock just melted," Rustle muttered. "I don't think we should wait. We have to find another way out before night. We'll lose all our light then."

Reluctantly, Feather nodded. She cast another uncertain glance at the crescent of light above. The slender stream of water plopped off the dark rock at her feet, splattered her toes, and trickled away to the distant spot of light far down the tunnel. Its splashes mingled with another sound... a flutter of wings.

"Shhh!" Rustle glanced over his shoulder. "Something's there."

Feather crouched down and grabbed a fistful of moss.

Rustle bounced the gemstone's beam around and upwards. It pierced the darkest shadows. Again, he heard a faint flutter.

At first it was only a soft *flap, flap, flap* which ruffled the air, but the next instant Rustle threw his arms over Feather's head as hundreds of bats whirled above their heads in a chaotic frenzy.

Feather screamed, "Nightraiders! They'll shred us to pieces!"

"Don't move!" Rustle shouted. "They can feel us moving, and they'll think we're crawlies!"

"Oh, no!" cried Feather. "They'll eat us!"

The big-eared bats eyes gleamed like crimson cinders in the dark. One bat after another brushed the Twigs' leafy heads with the tips of their wings and searched for any movement, which might signal a snack. The nightraiders would not leave as long as they sensed food was near.

Desperate to protect Feather, Rustle stood and swung his saver above his head so fast it became a spinning, sparkling disc. The nightraiders bounced their silent echoes off of it and swooped away. But after a while Rustle's strength ebbed. He whirled his saver slower and slower. The bats flew lower and closer, until their claws clutched at the stick and the Twigs hiding below it.

With a sudden burst, Feather grabbed Rustle, and yanked him underneath the falling stream of water. In an instant, they disappeared within the waterfall, and became invisible to the bats. Their echoes could not penetrate the surface of the water.

No longer having any treats to seek, the nightraiders swirled around for a while, and then rushed out of the tunnel.

"Ggggood thththinking," shivered Rustle. They remained huddled together in the cold water until the last bat left. "Iiii dddon't ththink Iii cccould hhave kkkept ththem offff usss much lllonger."

Feather wrapped her arms around Rustle and hugged him tight. Her swan feather drooped over them both. "I thhhink itttt'sss sssafffe nooww."

Rustle and Feather left the safety of the water. Sparkling beads dripped from every one of their leaves. They sat down on the floor, mopped their wet hair with moss, and huddled beneath their only beam of sunlight. The bright day was just above them in the forest which made the quiet of the tunnel even more eerie. But all was not quiet. More odd scratching noises floated around in the tunnel.

"What's that?" Rustle jumped at the noise.

Tilting her head to listen better Feather ventured a guess. "It's a beast without eyes, for sure, and it has really long claws. Probably thick, matted hair, too, so it stays warm down here. I'm sure it's a horrible beast that eats Twigs... especially Twigs that rustle and jump around. Like you, Rustle."

"Oh, that's real funny, Feather," Rustle laughed. "I bet it loves to eat Twigs that wear feathers stuck in their headbands, too! It would eat you first!"

"You think so?" Feather giggled. She contemplated the limp feather tucked in her headband. It dripped over her nose. She blew its tip up and down in rhythm with the falling water.

A low gurgle drifted from a nearby shadow.

Alarmed once again, Feather and Rustle pressed against the rock wall.

A hairless mole waddled from the shadows, and lapped the water. It was wrinkled and pink. The mole sniffed the air, sensing more than seeing it was not alone. It was about the size of a chipmunk although its head was larger. The mole's nose seemed to be splattered across its face. Finger-like stems wriggled from its nose. The stems twitched and stretched toward Feather and Rustle. It was eager to smell the other creatures which had also dropped into this strange place. The mole had no eyes, or maybe from lack of use they had just sunk deep in its skull. Long pink fingers and toes ended in sharp, curved claws, which clicked on the rock.

"What is it?" murmured Feather in Rustle's ear. "Should we fight it?"

Rustle shook his head, and held his saver across his chest. "It's a digger," he muttered. "They eat Twigs, so stay close in case I need to whack it. It must've fallen in here, too. It must be looking for a way out like us. Diggers are dangerous. Follow me." Rustle stepped sideways away from the digger, his back pressed against the wall.

Feather grabbed hold of Rustle's shoulder strap, and slid alongside him. She pulled the sharpened rock shard from her belt, held it tight in her fist, and raised it high. She remembered stories about diggers – creatures who lived in the ground and snatched Twigs from above as if they were juicy roots to devourer. In the woods where she grew up diggers were never seen, but they left tall mounds of dirt around their holes all over the meadows. It was dangerous for Twigs to fall into one. A digger can sense the slightest movement in its tunnel and they were fast. Before a Twig could crawl out and escape they'd be tackled and crunched in one bite. *No need to offer a digger an easy Twig meal,* decided Feather. *This digger will have to fight for its dinner.*

The mole wriggled closer.

WHACK! Rustle slammed his saver against the rock floor, hoping to frighten the mole away.

EEEEEKKKKK! It squeaked and seemed frightened. Still, it came closer and sniffed the air.

"It must be really hungry," Rustle whacked his saver again.

With a sudden rush, Feather darted to a clump of moss, grabbed it, and hurled it at the mole.

The digger whirled around. He snuffled the moss with interest, and nibbled it. Rustle and Feather bolted down the tunnel, and didn't stop running until the mole was out of sight.

"Whew," Rustle sighed. "I don't want to run into that beast again! We better find a way out of here before night falls and we lose the light. Let's just hope it's not any darker this way."

"Yes, let's hope," murmured Feather. *But we're going downhill. It's bound to get even darker now.*

Now the Twigs crept along with slow and careful steps. Feather kept one hand on her sharpened rock shard, and swept her gaze from side to side searching the shadows for movement. Rustle stared straight ahead, his eyes wide, straining to see in the dim light. One quiet footfall at a time, the Twigs stepped from one shaft of light to another, searching for a way out at each sunspot. But they could not find a way to climb up the smooth, curved walls. The tunnel led them even further below the forest floor. The spots of light grew fewer.

Nightraiders, bellycrawlers, diggers, and now no light, Rustle worried. *What else?*

Chapter Four

ALL THE OTHERS

At last it was quiet in the Old Seeder's hollow. The land waves had come and gone leaving the Twigs' haven looking more like the chaos of a bluebird's nest than a Twig's neat haven.

Leaf turned from watching the smoke spiral above Echo Peak, and waded through piles of crushed leaves. He brushed dried moss and dust from his hair. The dust billowed up into brilliant twinkles and floated out of the many high knotholes. Leaf surveyed their haven with dismay.

A thin branch shoved its way through a large knothole above the door. Its tiny pinecones littered the floor. Shattered robins-egg tea cups lay scattered. Their broken shells glittered like drops of dew. Bark carvings of creatures had fallen from shelves and lay splintered into weird-looking beasts. The mossy chair now blocked the tunnel leading to Mumma and Pappo's hollow. Drifting feathers from torn pillows settled on everything.

Leaf groaned. "What a mess!"

"Do you think there will be more land waves?" Fern wondered. She plucked feathers from Burba and Buddy's hair and few from her own.

"I don't dink so," replied Buddy, "Da Old Seeder's warm now 'cause it stopped shivering." He blew a feather off Fern's ear.

Burba braced himself on a stool just in case the trunk started to snap back and forth again. "Do 'ya think Mumma and Pappo got waved? Did the waves wave the river? Maybe it got Mumma and Pappo all wet, eh!" He grinned, delighted by the idea of his mother and father soaked by giant splashes from the Blue Band.

"Da waves got 'em!" giggled Buddy.

Leaf frowned at his little brothers. "You better just hope they're all right."

Burba and Buddy became solemn, but after a moment's pause they jumped up without another thought for Mumma and Pappo, and tripped over each other as they tried to catch the wispy feathers spiraling above their heads.

Leaf inspected his elbows and knees for splinters. Then he grabbed each of the twins by their shoulders, whirled them around, and inspected them too. At last he was satisfied. "Be careful running around all this broken stuff," he ordered the buds. "Go check your hollow and pick up the mess there." Leaf pulled long splinters from the shattered bark etchings, creating even more ghastly-looking beasts. "Guess we'll have to carve these all over again." He shook his head. Mumma would want new ones to hang on the walls. "Fern, how are you?" Leaf asked.

"Fine, I guess. That was so scary! I feel sorry for the poor creatures in the forest. How terrible it must be for them!" Fern added, "Maybe you better check on Whisper, Leaf. Do you think she's hurt?"

"Whisper's a smart chippie. She'd know to stay in her knothole, and hold on. But you're right. She might be afraid." Leaf answered, but now he could not help imagining the sweet chipmunk's whiskers quivering with fear. He stuck his head out the door, and shouted to a swirling knothole far below. "Hey, Whisper! Are you all right?"

CHRIRRPPCLK! Sharp chipmunk clicks and chitters, which sounded more like complaints than worries, ricocheted through the Old Seeder's limbs. *RIRRIPCHK! RIRRIPCHK!*

Leaf laughed, and looked back at Fern. "She's just fine. I think she's angry the waves interrupted her nap. Silly chippie."

The twins hunted for their stick dolls. Teeny stick arms and legs had broken off, so they had to be stuck together again. Burba discovered their old moss balls and began pelting Buddy with them.

Fern swept the broken shells into a pile until it was a glittering heap. She tossed berries in a half-crushed basket, and tried to straighten the shelves in the cupboards, but they didn't seem to want to be straightened. She paused struggling with the shelves, and stared at the slender branch sticking through the knothole above the door. "How are we ever going to get that out?"

Leaf shrugged. "Hey, it's kinda' pretty there. May be should just leave it."

Fern scowled at Leaf. "Don't be a nuthead. Help me push it back out," she ordered. "You jump on top and push it down, and I'll shove it out."

"Oh sure, and I'll get hurled across the hollow," protested Leaf, although he was glad to see Fern returning to her old, bossy self. "Let's just push it out together."

The buds rushed from their sleeping hollow and watched, just in case their big brother and sister got smashed. They didn't want to miss that. But with only a slight push the branch sprang out of the hollow. Disappointed, Buddy and Burba decided it would be fun to chase a crawlie twitching its way up the trunk. It sensed the twins stalking it, and crawled out of a tiny knothole.

Fern glanced out the half-open door. "Leaf, you should go check on the chompers and their dam. If it breaks..." her voice faded, and Fern could not help but look up toward the cliff, which rose high above the Old Seeder. The thought of the fast-flowing river – the Rushing Waters – bursting through the goliath beaver dam there was too frightening to consider.

Not very long ago the chompers had crammed their dam into the V-shaped cliff. Now only a slender waterfall cascaded down beneath the enormous barricade. The chompers protected the Twigs' homes by keeping the giant dam in good repair. The river swirled away from the cliff into a serene alpine lake, which filled a steep valley in the foothills of Echo Peak. It was an unusual spot for beavers to live, but it was proof of the strong friendship between the Twigs and goliath chompers.

"You should check them and the dam, Leaf," urged Fern.

Leaf just laughed. "If the dam broke, you'd know it by now!" But he wondered, too, if the chompers were all right. What about their homes? Leaf thought about the ferocious leader of the chomper colony – how scary he had seemed when they first met. Leaf smiled. *They're fine*. He shrugged off Fern's worry. *Their leader will keep them safe*.

Burba kicked a moss-ball and it whizzed by Fern's head. She ducked just in time.

"Uh, oh!" Buddy muttered. "You're gonna get it now, Burba."

Fern clapped her hands and snapped, "Come on, you two. Help me clean up now and I'll make mashcakes for you."

"Yay!" Buddy and Burba shouted. Right away the twins shoved crumpled leaves into corners, stuffed broken cedar fronds down tunnels, dragged the puffy chair into the center of the hollow, and kicked broken toys under it. Then they hurled pine nuts through the high knotholes, but most bounced off the walls. Burba took special delight in angling his pine nuts against the wall so they would whirl back and whizz past Buddy's head.

After dodging one too many pine nuts Buddy hid behind Leaf and stuck his tongue out at Burba. Buddy tugged on his big brother's elbow. "What about da Cappynuts, Leaf? And Mantru? And Bumper and Winkers and Puff and ..."

Leaf patted his brother on his head. "I can't check on everyone, Buddy. "We're fine, aren't we? I'm sure they're all fine, too."

Fern moved to the door, and gazed over the treetops to the fuzzy horizon which marked the Great Gorge. A wistful expression clouded her eyes. "Do you think Moon is all right?"

Leaf grinned. Ever since Fern had met Moon she spent most of her time wondering when she'd see him again. She constantly smashed the droopy leaves on her head to force them into an unnatural smooth style. She studied her solemn appearance in pools of water, and practiced smiling. With surprising courage, she often climbed to the tip of the Old Seeder, and sat gazing toward the gorge. Leaf wondered if Moon liked Fern, too.

Fern stepped near to Leaf and whispered so Buddy and Burba could not hear, "Why did it happen, Leaf? Is Echo Peak crumbling inside or something? Is it bursting open?"

"I don't know, Fern." Leaf spoke low, and shook his head. "I'm sure Mumma and Pappo will know why it's all happening."

A gray squirrel peeked through the knothole to take advantage of the unguarded Twig door. It reached toward the pine nuts scattered on the floor that lay just within its reach.

Fern grunted in disgust. "Don't you dare, you thieving chatters!" She grabbed a berry, aimed it at the squirrel's head, and hurled it, but it only skimmed over its nose. The squirrel sneered, chattered furiously at Fern, and then scurried after the berry, which was now bouncing off limbs on its way to the roots below.

Buddy yelled, "Yeah, don't ya' dare come in dis hollow, you dief!" He hurled another berry out the door at the disappearing squirrel.

Leaf laughed. "I guess Buddy takes after you, Fern!"

Fern stepped out on the porch branch with a pine nut ready to throw just in case more chatters lurked nearby. Seeing none, she grabbed the stiff broom beside the door. In a flurry of dust the hollow was soon clean. She swept the last of the crushed leaf-drawings from the porch, and paused to enjoy the early morning glow of Echo Peak.

The last, pink streaks of thin clouds stretched across the sky like skinny Twig fingers. The warm rays of the sun frayed the mist. The High Waterfall's distant echoes splashed on the cliffs.

Fern wondered aloud, "Maybe we should go away for a while... just until we're sure it's safe again. Maybe we could go to the Great Gorge..." Fern's voice faded with embarrassment when she caught the wicked gleam in Leaf's eyes. She blushed and turned away.

"Oh, yes, good idea," Leaf teased her. "Let's go right now! Mumma and Pappo won't even miss us. And you can ask Moon if he's met any Twigs as wonderful as you. I bet there aren't any as spindly or colorful, either! He's probably just sitting around hoping you show up again. Leaf nodded toward the knothole. "Good idea! Come on, let's go right now!"

"Oh, stop it!" Fern frowned, turned away, and then sighed. She remembered Moon's shy smile and pale, pale eyes. *Wonder if he thinks about me at all?* Fern plucked dried moss out of her golden hair, and smashed the leaves flat on her head. *Well, if he ever shows up here again at least my leaves will be smooth.*

"Mashcakes," Leaf called out. "Time to make mashcakes. The day isn't flowing any slower!"

CHAPTER FIVE

YIPPERS & CAPPYNUTS

Far away from where the Old Seeder stood sentinel over the forest, and from where two chippies wandered down a deer path on their way to find Leaf, the South Forest came to an abrupt end. Only creatures with wings challenged the chasm called the Great Gorge. Twigs watched with awe as birds flew from one distant tree tip to another. In its depths snaked the Canyon River, so remote and turbulent Twigs grew dizzy at its sight.

An ancient log bridge once existed for earth-bound creatures to cross the gorge. That was when swarms of barkbiters devoured the trees in the North Forest. But they, along with the log bridge were caught in a firestorm, scorched to ashes, and fell into the Canyon River. Still, the Twigs of the South Forest knew it was only a matter of time before barkbiters recovered and found a way to reach the south rim, so young Twigs like the

Cappynut twins Ruffle and Tuffle became guards and protected the South Forest from barkbiters.

A few seasons ago a family of North Forest Twigs escaped the barkbiters and fire. A silver-haired Twig with gray eyes named Star, her pale brother Moon, her grandfather PapaMook, six Twig babes, and an assortment of loyal, odd creatures — stickytoes and a looksalot — fled to the South Forest across the log bridge.

Now Star lived with her family in a new tree haven at the edge of the Great Gorge. She often climbed to its tip, and gazed across the South Forest at the only tree poking above the forest of treetops. The tree's silhouette was majestic against the glaring-white cone of Echo Peak, and seeing the Old Seeder gave Star hope she might soon see Leaf again, for it was Leaf who had rescued her and her family from the barkbiters and firestorm.

Today, however, Star had taken all the Twig babes on a picnic. She lounged in a sunny meadow and watched the sprouts play just a little too close to a shallow creek. Fearful they might be swept away by the bubbling water she admonished them with a pleasant, patient voice, "Breeze, Moss, Sand, stay out of the water! Cone and Mist, I think you have enough mud on your faces, already! Pool, I expect you to keep an eye on the younger sprouts. Keep them away from the water, please!"

Three orange-spotted salamanders named Click, Chirp, and Crunch tilted their heads at the sound of Star's voice for they loved her. They sprawled in the muck of the creek by a rotting log, and licked their eyes with long, pink tongues. Together they slipped from slimy, mossy rocks into the cool creek. It was easier to sneak up on crawlies from under the water. They took turns flicking water beetles into each other's orange mouths.

On the branches of a vine maple at the clearing's edge two imposing chameleons, and friends of Star, slept with their tails curled up over their backs. Their two-toed hands gripped slender leaf stems. One of the looksalot had turned a dappled putty shade like the tree bark. His name was Veil. The other looksalot shimmered a blue sapphire color like the sky, so of course, Star had named her Sky.

At the edge of the meadow a starling with fluorescent feathers and bright-yellow legs ripped up stones with his sharp claws. He was an irritating, snobby tooler. Star's grandfather PapaMook had rescued him and named him Pesky. Pesky was especially clever which in his case made him suspicious and arrogant. Pesky flipped over another stone. A beetle was shocked by the sunlight, and in desperation scrambled to reach the shade of a nearby rock. Delighted, Pesky hopped on it, speared the crawlie with his beak, smashed it against a stone, and gobbled up the pieces with a satisfied burp.

The Cappynut twins, Ruffle and Tuffle, had also been invited to the picnic, although they were still on Gorge Patrol. No barkbiters had been seen for seasons now, but Ruffle and Tuffle took their duty seriously, in between long naps, berry picking, and picnics. They were silly-looking, lanky Twigs with fluffy, colorful feathers stuck in their belts. Tuffle's feathers were wood-duck gold and Ruffle's were jay-blue.

Now, hoping to impress Star with their prowess, the twins crept among huge deer ferns with slingshots held high, and stalked a purple dragonfly. A bag of pebbles hung open from their belts, ready to re-load their slingers in an instant. Ruffle and Tuffle were quite skilled with their sling-shots, but perhaps not as skilled as their paps Sapper, who lounged nearby in the sun chewing on grass stems, and ignoring his annoying sons.

Sapper was usually found within arguing distance of PapaMook, Star's grandpaps. The two old Twigs occupied their time with endless discussions about forest skills and the challenges of raising Twig sprouts. They watched Ruffle and Tuffle stalk the dragonfly, and agreed the twins' excellent hunting techniques still left much to criticize.

With an unexpected dive behind a fern, Ruffle yanked Tuffle down beside him, and hissed, "Look. *It's* back again."

"*It?*" asked Tuffle. He could barely see anything. His curled, dusty leaves fell in a bunch over his eyes. Like his twin brother only his pointed nose could be seen above his lopsided grin. The rest of his face was a tangle of leaves. Tuffle parted the fronds of the fern for a better look. "Where?"

Ruffle jabbed his elbow in his brother's side.

"Whad'ja poke me for?" protested Tuffle.

"Shhhh! It'll hear us!" hissed Ruffle.

A log's length from the twins the fuzzy tips of a coyote pup's ears twitched back and forth just above a patch of grass.

"What'd ya think it want here? Do ya think it eats stickytoes?" worried Tuffle.

"Nay, yippers don't eat stickytoes," replied Ruffle with a superior tone. "Don't you know anything, nuthead?

But they might eat a tooler." With a sly look at Tuffle, he added, "Or they might eat you just to sharpen their teeth!"

"Ya mean like splinter me?" asked Tuffle with an anxious glance at his brother.

Ruffle snorted. *My brother is so easy to fool.* "Come on, let's get closer," he urged Tuffle. "Bet we can scare it away with our slingers." He pulled out his slingshot and a perfect, round pebble.

The Cappynuts crawled on hands and knees toward the bobbing head of the pup. If it weren't for their gold and blue feathers trembling above the grass tips, they might have been invisible. At last they could see the pale fur of the pup's head.

Nervous, Tuffle whispered, "What'll we do now? Ya gonna smack it on its head and scare it away?"

"Na," answered Ruffle. "I'm gonna whack it between the eyes and knock it out. Then we can drag it to Star. She'll tell us what to do with it."

Tuffle stopped crawling and sat up. "I don't think you should do that, Ruffle. Star don't like us whackin' creatures with our slingers. She'll be mad at us."

"Star doesn't want us to *smack* things," retorted Ruffle. "Whacking is just fine. I'm gonna whack it, not smack it."

"Smacking and whacking is the same thing, you nut-head!" accused Tuffle. "How you gonna smack something without whacking it?"

Ruffle stood up. He crossed his arms, and squared off against his brother. "You don't know anything! Look!" Ruffle took aim at a pine cone dangling above them on a fir tree. With expert precision he stretched back the slingshot's string, let the pebble fly, and chuckled as the pine cone whizzed off the branch and sailed through the sky.

"That's *smacking* not *whacking!*" explained Ruffle with a superior expression. Right away he loaded another pebble and shot a cone hanging right above Tuffle's head. The cone exploded into pieces and showered Tuffle. "If I wanted to *whack* somethin', I'd do *that!* See the difference?" Ruffle sneered at his brother.

With a sour face Tuffle picked pieces of pine cone out of his hair. "Right. So you wanna' whack it then?"

Ruffle nodded. "Right!"

With a startled expression Tuffle looked over Ruffle's head. His eyes widened. He hissed, "Well, you better whack it right now!"

The coyote pup stood above the Cappynuts with curious eagerness. Breathy, snuffling snorts blew Ruffles' hair up. Stunned, Ruffle and Tuffle froze. Two more coyote pups pounced from the grass, and stood panting beside the first. Their pink tongues flopped from the side of their mouths, below their shivering whiskers. All beamed with delight.

"YIPPERS!" screamed Ruffle.

At once the twins bolted from the meadow and into the protection of the tall trees in the forest.

The three pups bounded after them. "*YIP, YIP, YIP, YIP!*" Their merry barks echoed among the trees and shadows.

Ruffle and Tuffle took turns grabbing each other's arms and legs, and yanking the other behind as each tried to be the first to reach the closest branch in the nearest tree.

YIP, YIP, YIP, YIP! The pups' bounced after the Cappynuts with clumsy, off-balanced leaps. Then they rolled into an excited ball of muffled yips and protests. The yippers untangled themselves just as Ruffle and Tuffle scrambled up the trunk to the branch, and clung there out of reach.

The coyote pups jumped up and down beneath Ruffle and Tuffle, yelping, "*YIP, YIP, YIP!*" Finally, they sat beneath the tree, impatient and unhappy, and howled teeny, mournful howls.

"Smack 'em!" shouted Tuffle.

Ruffle fumbled with his slingshot, but he was shaking too much to load a pebble. At that moment the Cappynuts noticed a rustling in the ferns along the deer path near the tree. On silent paws the graceful coyote mum appeared. With joy the pups bounced around and urged her to climb up and capture the Twigs. She quieted the pups with patient nuzzles, and shoved them back into the forest shadows. The yipper family left.

"You ruined it," complained Ruffle as he slid down the trunk to land in the moss. "You made too much noise. I could 'a whacked it, for sure."

"Oh, yeah?" challenged Tuffle. "What were you gonna do with the other two then? Kiss 'em?"

The Cappynut twins argued all the way back to the sunlit meadow. When they reached the picnic, they heard the Twig babes pleading with PapaMook.

"Story! We want a story, PapaMook!"

Ruffle and Tuffle hurried. *A story!*

"Tell us a story, PapaMook!" entreated the babes. It was their rest time and stories always helped the daily pause in their play flow faster.

Star stepped between the babes and her old grandpaps. "First, you need to go search for some berries!

Here." Star hung a little basket from each babe arm. "Off you go. Don't be long, now. And bring back some pine nuts, too."

The Twig sprouts wandered off searching for treats to enjoy during story time.

The Cappynuts slowed their steps.

"Uh, we should probably guard the forest some more, eh?" murmured Ruffle. "Just while they're getting the treats, eh?"

"Yeah, berry-hunting is for babes not guards," agreed Tuffle. "Let's take a nap. We gotta' rest up if we're gonna help 'em eat berries and nuts."

"Yep," nodded Ruffle. "Better rest first."

They slumped against a thick plant with tall, blue flowers and crossed their legs. Soon their snores distracted the butterflies from the blue blossoms.

Neither noticed a strange Twig sneaking into the meadow. He had thick hemlock fronds for hair and appeared more stump-like than a Twigs' usual stick figure. He carried a taut, flaxen rope draped over his shoulder and across his chest. He gripped it tight to keep it still. He paused by the slumbering Cappynuts, waited for a particularly long snore, and then crept past. He crawled closer to the picnic until he could hear Star's voice drifting among the dandelion fluff.

"PapaMook. Sapper. Listen," Star spoke in her usual soft way as if she were talking to tiny Twig sprouts. "I climbed to the very tip of our tree this morning. I could see far away – all the way across the South Forest to Echo Peak. The air was so clear I noticed something strange on the white mountain. The pink light from the morning sun made it look as if a huge, great big bubble was sticking out of the side of Echo Peak. Do you think it was just the pink morning light, or could there really be a big bubble there?"

The two old Twigs perked up their ears.

"Whadda' ya see, again?" asked PapaMook. "Was it an orange light 'stead of pink, maybe? Orange means a storm's comin', ya know."

"No, no, purple means a storm's coming," contradicted Sapper.

"No, no, orange," retorted PapaMook.

"Purple!" Sapper jutted out his chin and glared.

Star interrupted, "Please, please, it doesn't matter if it's pink or orange or purple or green or blue...." Star voice faded away. She sat quiet for a moment, and then tried to explain, again. "It was like a big lump on the side of Echo Peak. Like a giant bubble was blowing up inside the mountain. So strange..."

Sapper tapped his mouth, lost in thought.

PapaMook grinned like he knew a secret. "I know a story about a bubble on Echo Peak."

"You do not!" declared Sapper. "You're just making it up."

"I do, too!" countered PapaMook. "It's all about how Echo Peak had a bubble... just like when a pond croaker makes a bubble in its throat to croak." PapaMook winked at Star. "The oldest Twigs in the forest said the bubble on Echo Peak got bigger and bigger and bigger until it blew up the mountain!" He grinned with delight at Star's shocked expression.

Sapper sneered, "A croaker's throat doesn't blow up. It just lets the wind out with a giant burp." He sat back with a smug look on his face. "Besides, you just made up that story anyway. I never heard of such a thing." He patted Star's hand to reassure her. "Echo Peak's not gonna blow up, now little one. PapaMook's just makin' it up."

"Am not!" PapaMook sounded angry.

"Anyway, that's not much of a story, you old knot," said Sapper with no small amount of scorn.

"Well, some I heard the bubble got really big like this. And land waves started rocking the forest back and forth and back and forth!" PapaMook held out his hands wide, and waved them up and down. "But after a while the land waves stopped and the bubble just shrunk up and melted away. Echo Peak never croaked." He took Star's chin in his hand. "I think that's what happens, little one. When there's a bubble on Echo Peak it just goes away. You keep an eye on it. You'll see."

"Hmmpff," grunted Sapper. "Croakin' mountains. Land waves. Bubbles on Echo Peak. Nonsense."

Star ignored them. *Land waves?* She hadn't felt any land waves here. She picked up a broken sliver from a stone and scribbled in the dirt. She drew Echo Peak with a lumpy bulge sticking out of its side. *I wonder if Leaf can see the bubble? No,* she decided. *Probably not. It's probably just my imagination.* Still, Star felt uneasy.

The strange, stealthy Twig with hemlock hair knelt in the grass and watched Star gather the Twig babes from the honeysuckle thickets, and shoo them back to the patched picnic covies lying flat on the grass. Star turned to stare in his direction as if she sensed another presence in the meadow. But Hemlock knew she'd never spot him. He hid well. He was clever and skillful. Just in case, he sunk lower in the grass.

The tips of the Cappynut twins' feathers trembled in rhythm with their snores. Star watched the two sleeping in the shade and grinned. *Some guards! They'll wake up for treats!* The Twig sprouts brought her all their tasty treasures. She spilled the baskets onto the covies, and divided them into neat piles before each giggling babe.

Hemlock relaxed, adjusted his rope to be more comfortable, and hid beneath the curling tip of the tall grass. He knew the sprouts would soon rest on their mossy pillows and the old Twig they called PapaMook would tell a rambling story. He plucked a grass stem to chew while he waited. He was curious about these new Twigs who had moved from the north, and now lived so near his own dark forest full of dripping moss and scattered sunlight. This past season Hemlock had returned again and again to spy on them.

Wonder why the little sprouts are so happy? Hemlock envied them – always giggling and chasing one another. There were no other young Twigs to play with in Hemlock's forest, and so he was always alone. Sometimes these new Twig babes played in the creek and threw mud at each other. The slender, silver-haired Twig called Star cared for them all. Her brother Moon helped, too. They seemed so happy... so normal... like Twigs should be. But still, Hemlock worried about them.

His Branch of Twigs – the Hemlock Twig Branch – believed their suffocating trees with their heavy, moss-draped branches were better than all other trees. Hemlocks guarded their dripping forest with a jealous passion, and moved restlessly about searching for strange Twigs who trespassed down their secret paths. Angry and violent, they attacked in the dark, hurling cones like hailstones and thrashing sticks like whips until the creatures in the forest fled before their rage.

Hemlock knew his Branch of Twigs could easily mob Star's tree-haven in the night, and drive her family into the gorge. Hemlock shivered. Their vengeful, merciless nature frightened even him.

Star glanced over her shoulder, and squinted in the bright light. *Did I see something move there?* She watched the tips of the deep grass surrounding them. The tips would betray any movement, but only the pale clover quivered at the touch of honeybees. The edge of the meadow melted into the forest. Star shrugged, and turned away.

Hemlock rested beneath the tall stalks of grass, closed his eyes, and waited for PapaMook's story. He wished he could tell Star he was different from the others in his

Branch. That he would never chase her away. That he would warn her of danger... even protect her and her family. But Hemlock knew he would never tell her anything at all.

Like all Hemlock Twigs, he never spoke.

Chapter Six

THE LAKE IS SINGING

Above the Old Seeder a goliath beaver dam was stuffed in the cleft of a high, sheer cliff. Stacks and stacks of logs packed together with mud rose above a slender ribbon of water, which fluttered down the cliff into a cool, deep pool. Behind the dam a river rushed into a sapphire-colored, alpine lake. The lake's quiet waters reflected the trembling leaves of birch and aspen trees clinging to its shores.

The lake stirred. A flat, black nose stuck up just above the surface of the water. A goliath beaver paddled toward the shore. He was swift and graceful even though his back legs were crooked and weak. His flat, oval-shaped tailed steered him with powerful strokes. He was the leader of a chomper colony of goliath beavers, and his name was Slapper. Twigs did not know this since Twigs did not understand chompers, nor did chompers understand Twigs. Still, they became friends.

Slapper and his mate Patty were the oldest in the colony. Not long ago Patty gave birth to two new pups, Bubbles and Slick. They were destined to be as huge and intimidating as their father and mother, but for now their tiny bodies were nurtured with love, pride, and warm milk. Their older sisters, Splash and Splatter – also enormous beavers – smothered the new kits with affection. By tender nudges and nuzzles they taught Bubbles and Slick how to swim in and out of the tunnels of their lodge.

Soon, Splash and her mate Birchbite would raise their own family, and Splatter and her mate Clacker would have theirs, too. Each had already constructed their own round lodge near the lakeshore. The walls of the lodges had been stuffed with mud, rocks, grass, and sticks. A small hole poked through the top for fresh air and an occasional shaft of sunlight.

Slapper pulled himself onto a flat rock just above the surface of the lake. The lookout was near his lodge, and offered him an excellent view of the woods, shore, and lake. Slapper was injured long ago, and his legs grew weaker as each season passed, so now he stayed in the water or his lodge. The others had learned their skills well, and no longer needed his help chomping trees for the dam. Still, Slapper guarded his colony with brutal vigilance. Two sharp *WHACKS!* of his tail signaled danger, and as quick as his signal echoed off the cliffs, the whole chomper colony would dive underwater and shelter in their lodges until Slapper signaled all was safe. Cougars, foxes, and other prowlers knew to keep their distance from the sinister-looking beaver. Even eagles – enormous and silent – floated by without a glance at the pups splashing in the water. None challenged Slapper. And so all the beavers enjoyed the sunny morning, groomed in the warmth of the rays, and left guarding the colony to their ferocious leader.

This is a perfect lookout, Slapper reflected as he groomed his whiskers.

But even Slapper could not guard them from the earthquakes which shook the ridge above the alpine lake and hurled boulders down into its still waters.

BOOM! BOOM! CRACK! SPLASH!

In an instant all the chompers dove into the lake, and swam to Slapper and Patty's lodge. There they huddled together, shivering and confused. Slapper stood guard at the tunnel entrance, but he did not know what might come up through the lake to threaten them.

BOOM! BOOM! CRACK! SPLASH!

Boulders crashed into the lake. Violent waves smashed trees on the shore. The hard-packed walls in Slapper's lodge cracked and twisted. The lake grew still. The mud walls held.

Slapper swam from the lodge, and slid onto his lookout rock. With the eye of an experienced engineer, he calmly surveyed the damaged landscape. Huge boulders had broken off the cliffs and rolled into the water. They had missed their lodge-homes although piles of rubble now blocked Slapper's view of Splatter and Clacker's den. Many trees lay smashed and splintered on the shore.

Splatter and Clacker must build another den closer to the others now, Slapper decided right away. *But first we must inspect the dam.* He watched his family swim from his lodge and waddle onshore. Right away they examined the smashed trees spread out like a picnic with eager surprise.

Change is good, Slapper reminded himself. *Chompers make change. Only then are their dams and ponds full of life. If there is no change, there is no life.*

A few birch trees snapped by the quake lay crisscrossed near the dam. Slapper considered the easy pickings. *Easy to strip. The work will be good schooling for Bubbles and Slick.*

Eerrreeechch... A whisper... a high-pitched shriek floated through the water and reached Slapper's keen ears. Only he heard it. Without hesitation he slapped the water once with his tail. *WHACK!* It was as if a lightning bolt struck the lake, yet the slap was an alert not a warning.

Patty shoved Bubbles and Slick underwater and pushed them up the lodge tunnel to the den. Birchbite and Clacker sat up rigid and sniffed the air. Splash and Splatter dove into the lake and a moment later slipped onto the rock by their father. They sat alert, staring in different directions. The water was so still the sunlight's glare reflected off the lake and blinded them. After a moment the four young chompers fixed their gaze on their leader, waiting for him to give them direction. Slapper tilted his head and listened, so the others did, too, and it was then they all heard it.

Eerrreeechch... Eerrreeechch...

Slapper scowled. *What is that? A song? Singing?* A faded memory nagged him.... a memory of his first home with Patty where his daughters had met their mates. They called it the Spreading Pond. One night he had heard a strange trickling noise creeping through the murky water. It sang like a warped melody. *A song in* the pond..., Slapper remembered. The noise had irritated him, and so he had searched for it. When he found the source of the trickle, he was overwhelmed by a flash flood. It shattered their lodge home and destroyed their pond. Slapper learned the melody meant danger.

This song is different. Slapper concentrated. *Like the wail of a wounded creature... crying in pain.* Slapper felt his skin crawl. *It's in the water. Deep in the lake.* He took a huge gulp of air and dove toward the deepest part of the lake to investigate.

Birchbite, Clacker, Splatter, and Splash plunged into the lake, and hurried after Slapper. Deeper and deeper they swam until they reached him.

Slapper was floating motionless in the water, listening. His goliath body cast a massive shadow on the bright-colored pebbles of the lake bottom. His broad tail swept back and forth in slow rhythm with the shrill, rhythmic song.

The song is coming from below the lake, Slapper realized with surprise. *And there's something else... the water feels warm.*

The chompers could not know that far below the lake sluggish molten rock curled in the belly of Echo Peak. It pressed against the huge granite slabs, which had trapped it for thousands of seasons. The grating rocks sang songs of protest as they cracked, but the magma could not be held back. Only the chompers could hear the shrieks from the rocks. Only they felt the water warming as the river of fire rose up toward the heart of Echo Peak.

Slapper floated with his hands curled up against his chest, his eyes closed. Clacker, Birchbite, Splash, and Splatter floated alongside their leader, trusting he would signal what next to do.

Slapper drifted. *It's like a great beast is moving under the lake... a great beast.* In the instant it takes a heart to skip a beat Slapper realized their danger. *We must leave!* With a mighty push of his tail, Slapper propelled himself to the surface, and in a shower of silver waves burst above the lake's surface.

A moment later Splash, Birchbite, Splatter, and Clacker exploded from the water, too. Frantic, they scanned the splashing waves for their leader.

Slapper had already reached Patty, and at once she knew. *We must leave!*

Chapter Seven

Mantru of the Long Ice

"Buddy! Burba! Be quiet!" Fern whispered. "Leaf, do you hear that?" Her eyes grew wide. She backed into the hollow, and hid behind one of the roots sticking from the knothole door.

Alarmed, Leaf tiptoed to the door. A screeching echo like the mangled squawking of angry jays bounced off the cliff wall. It twisted its way up through the Old Seeder's branches.

With a gasp Burba threw his patched blanket over his head. Then he grabbed Buddy's arm and yanked his brother under his covie, too. They sat shivering with their brown toes sticking out from under the worn blanket.

"It's a beast!" cried Fern. "It's a beast!" Then she remembered Whisper, tucked away in her chipmunk den below them. "Oh, Leaf! Whisper is down there! You must save her!"

"Whisper will know to hide," Leaf replied. He slammed shut the door, and stood on tiptoe with his nose pressed against the window. In a low voice he cautioned, "Shhh! It's coming right for the Old Seeder!"

EEAAAAFEEFF! BUEEEEEE!

The beast's horrible squealing grew louder. It tramped down the deer path which led directly from Slapper's dam and the High Falls to the Old Seeder.

EAAAAFEEFF! URRRRRBAAAA!

There was a strange rhythm to its cries.

Leaf hissed, "Be still! It's coming closer. Shhh! It's right below in the roots! Fern, do you think it can climb trees?"

Normally Fern was the expert on all wildlife in the forest, but now she only stared back at Leaf with huge, round eyes. She threw her arms over her squirming, mumbling brothers. "Buddy, Burba, you must be still!"

EEAAFEEFF! URRRBAAA! BUEEEE!

Buddy screamed, "Da beast is coming! Da beast is coming!"

Burba stuck his head out of a rip in his covie and shrieked at Leaf, "Throw something at it! Throw Mumma's chair!"

"Drow domding! Drow domding!" bawled Buddy. "Drow da mashcakes!"

Burba hissed at Buddy, "No, don't throw the mashcakes! We want the mashcakes."

"Oh, right." Buddy nodded and yelled, "Don't drow the mashcakes!"

"Be sticks!" ordered Fern to the buds.

Beneath the covie Buddy and Burba twisted themselves into the shape of bushes as they had been taught to do when danger was near.

The next moment Leaf stood up, grinned, and laughed. He flung open the door and waved to Fern to come look. "It's a beast all right. A beast whose singing will scare all the creatures in the forest! Hey, Buddy and Burba. Come say hello to the beast – our old friend Mantru!"

"Mantru!" the buds shouted together. At once Buddy and Burba tossed off the covie, and tumbled over one another to be the first to reach the porch-branch. Mantru! Mantru!" they yelled.

"Allllloooo!" shrieked a creaky voice from the branches below. "At last I found you."

Leaf laughed, and tugged Fern toward the door. "It's only Mantru from the Long Ice. You know. That old Willow Twig that lives up there and takes care of the snow creatures on Echo Peak. Come on, and meet him, Fern. He's not so scary. Really!"

Fern peeked over the edge of the porch, and gasped. She could just make out Mantru's weird-looking figure climbing up the Old Seeder.

An old, grizzled Twig who was far too tall and lanky for an ordinary Twig huffed and puffed his way up from limb to limb through the early morning mist. His face was knotted into twists from many long seasons spent fighting the bitter winds, which blew across the vast glacier called the Long Ice. He wore a goat-hair coat so large it covered his toes. Wispy, orange leaves drooped off his head and framed his beady, ruby-colored eyes. Fern recognized the helmet he wore. It was same sort of helmet Leaf wore when had gone to the Long Ice in search of his runaway brothers. The helmet had two sharp, black goat horns poking through it. Fern was impressed. Mantru looked like a giant, angry goat climbing up their tree.

The twins giggled. Leaf shouted encouragement to help the old Willow Twig make it all the way up to their haven. Mantru complained the entire way.

With a grin Leaf muttered over his shoulder to Fern, "At least he stopped singing."

Mantru finally reached the porch and stood towering over the twins. Buddy and Burba hugged the old

Twig's knees and he patted them fondly on their heads. Still, Mantru kept up a steady stream of complaints. "What a nutty haven! Only Old Seeder Twigs would live so high! Your haven is higher than the clouds! Look at that!" He pointed at a wisp of fog floating below. "The clouds are hiding everything below you, don't ya' know? And your forest is so thick with trees how can ya' see anything anyway? I had ta' shout and sing all the way from the Long Ice, so you'd know I was comin'! Nutty! Nutty!" Mantru paused to take a breath and stare up at the branches above them. He leaned far back, but could not spot the Old Seeder's tip. "This old tree is almost as tall as Echo Peak," he admitted.

Leaf stood with his hands on his hips. He beamed with pride. "That's exactly what makes it the best place to live in the forest. Anyway, it's better than living in a cave on Echo Peak with a bunch of nutty creatures." Leaf chuckled and hugged the old Twig. "Mantru! It's great to see you! Whatever made you leave the Long Ice? I can't believe you came all this way. How did you find us?"

"Well, Leaf, your tree *is* the tallest tree in the forest, just like you told me. And, anyway, there's only one path down the ridge, past the lake, and over the chomper dam. I figured if I sang loud enough you'd hear me."

Mantru leaned over and grasped Leaf's shoulders. "My young friend, it's good to see you!" His knotted face wrinkled up with a smile so huge his ruby eyes could barely be seen.

"That was singing?" murmured Fern.

"Ah, this must be Fern!" Mantru reached out with an arm so long and willowy his hand seemed to float through the air toward Fern. He patted her head.

Buddy and Burba's excitement could not be contained. "Did'ja bring Winkers and Puff and Poppy and Flip and da squeakers, too?" they cried out.

"What about Bumper?" Buddy shouted. "Did da ridgerunners come, too? Are dey here, too?"

Burba interrupted, "Hey, Mantru, wanna' build a trap for our hollow? We could make a great trap, don't ya' think? Hey, did ya' slide down the Long Ice on your ridgerunner coat?"

Mantru nodded. "All my friends are here. All except the ridgerunners herd, of course. But the tiniest ridgerunner stayed with me to help carry my creature friends in their baskets." He winked at the twins. "I think he wants to see you, too."

"Bumper's here? Great!" shouted Burba.

"All da others are down dere?" asked Buddy. He knelt on the porch-branch and peered over the edge.

"Yes, they're down there in their baskets, see?" Mantru pointed down through the mist. From the overturned baskets a pika, two snowshoe hares, teeny mice, and a horned lark wandered about in the roots eating blossoms and moss. Nearby, a tiny, white mountain goat nibbled on blue blossoms.

At once Burba scooted backwards down the trunk. "Come on, Buddy!" he yelled.

"You be careful climbing down!" Leaf shouted after Burba.

"Can we go see dem?" Buddy asked Leaf.

"Yes, let's go!" cried Fern. She dove into the haven and returned a moment later with shoulder sling full of berries and nuts. She loved the stories Leaf had told of Poppy, Puff, Winkers, the squeakers, and the odd bird Flip. "Come on, Buddy. You can show me your friends from the Long Ice."

Mantru called after them, "Be careful of Poppy! That snowyshoe is as grumpy as always!"

Mantru squeezed in through the knothole to the hollow, and sat down cross-legged. "My, my, what a nice hollow you have. Those sprouts have grown so much taller! Bet they're still trouble, eh?"

Leaf snorted. "As always! Tea, Mantru? Want some berry mashcakes?" He searched for an unbroken eggshell cup. He found one and blew off the dust.

"Wonderful! Yes, both please." Mantru sighed and wondered when was the last time he had had any tea or mashcakes. "Echo Peak is so shaky now I can barely make tea anymore. And oh, how it stinks! Smelly air creeps from cracks in the rocks all over the mountain. Yechh!"

Leaf looked up, surprised. "Is that why you came down? It's too stinky up there? Do you want to stay here with us? You are always welcome, you know." He quickly warmed mint tea in sunbeams streaming through a high knothole. He picked up a smashed mashcake from the floor, checked to see if it was too dirty to eat, and then broke off a piece for himself and Mantru.

"Too bad the ridgerunner's didn't come," chatted Leaf. "I'd love to see their amazing leader again."

Grateful for the food, Mantru slurped the tea down in one gulp, and swallowed the mashcake whole. "The ridgerunner herd left Echo Peak when all the land waves began. They are traveling along the ridge to Thunder Peak." He waved in the direction of a far-away mountain near the western edge the great Gorge.

"Yes, I know that ridge," nodded Leaf. He remembered a sweet hummer named Shimmer who had saved him from three bellycrawlers there.

Glittering sunbeams bounced about the hollow. The leaves on Mantru's head glowed like an orange halo. He brushed away the cake crumbs, placed his hands on his knees, and motioned to Leaf to sit nearby. "I'm going to Thunder Mountain, too," he grunted. "Echo Peak stinks so bad I can hardly sleep. And it never stops shaking! I can't even stack my baskets anywhere."

Leaf giggled. He could just imagine the stacks and stacks of carefully woven baskets in Mantru's cave falling on his head while he slept.

"Hmmpf," grunted Mantru, a little offended at not being taken seriously.

"Um, why does it stink, Mantru?" Leaf asked politely.

"How would I know?" the old Twig replied. "All I know is there are cracks all over the Long Ice, and where there are cracks a foul, stinky smell seeps out. It makes the snow creatures so sick they're all leaving. Big chunks of ice are melting and sliding off the mountain, too. I've seen whole pieces disappear right into the cracks. Why, hunks of ice nearly crushed me on my way down."

"Is it really that bad?" ask Leaf in disbelief.

Mantru leaned so far forward his nose almost touched Leaf's. His gaze was intense. "I came to warn you… you and your family. I think the Long Ice is gonna slide right off the mountain and smother the forest. You and your Old Seeder are gonna be smashed flat! You better tell your Pappo and Mumma to get you all out of here quick!"

Leaf gasped, "Really?" Leaf knew Mantru had lived on the vast glacier most of his life. The old Twig knew more about Echo Peak than any Twig who lived in the forest could possibly know. *He is probably right,* Leaf realized. *But leave our home?* "Um, when do you think we should we go?"

Mantru shook his head. "I don't know but all the creatures are already running away. On my way here I even saw the giant chompers climb down their dam and slide over the waterfall. Didn't you hear that big one slapping the water in the pool? It was like he was trying to warn the whole forest. then they slipped on down the stream toward the Wide Valley."

Leaf's eyes grew large. "The chompers left? I guess I couldn't hear anything over the twins shouting all the time."

"You know if chompers leave their dam then whatever is gonna happen will happen soon," urged Mantru. "I think the chompers are trying to escape to the Blue Band.

Leaf jumped up. "I have to warn Pappo and Mumma right away! They're at the fork of the Blue Band! Mantru, come with us. We can build rafts and float down the river like the chompers, and get away from Echo Peak before the Long Ice crushes us all." Leaf choked on his words. "I'm sure you're right, Mantru. It's not safe here anymore. We have to leave the Old Seeder."

With a sad look Mantru nodded, and patted Leaf's head in sympathy. "Yes, better leave fast like the chompers, my friend. Go find your Pappo and Mumma. I can't go with you. I must take the little ridgerunner back to his family on Thunder Peak, so I will escape along the ridge."

Leaf glanced around the haven. *Leave the Old Seeder... our haven....* "Yes, yes, we better leave right away."

The old Willow Twig's eyes filled with sorrow. "I know what it's like to leave a home forever, Leaf, but sometimes we have no choice." With that Mantru stood up, or as much as he could stand in the hollow, patted Leaf's shoulder, and stepped out of the haven. He sighed, "I left my Willow Tree haven when I lost my family in the terrible flood. Now I must leave my cave home on the Long Ice. At least I have friends with me this time...

Winkers, Flip, Puff, Poppy, the squeakers, and the little ridgerunner Bumper. I only hope the other creatures on Echo Peak will find safety, too." As if to hide his tears, Mantru took a sudden interest in smoothing stray goat hairs on the cuff of his coat.

Sadness filled Leaf for his old, creaky friend. He wished to comfort him, but could only think to say, "There will be ice caves on Thunder Peak, Mantru. You'll find another haven there."

Mantru gave Leaf an odd glance. He grunted, "The ice is melting everywhere now, my friend. It won't last on Thunder Peak either. The seasons are changing." He gave Leaf a wink. "But don't worry so much. Change is good for Twigs, Leaf. That's how we find new ways to grow."

"Yes," Leaf agreed, although he felt like it was too much change, all at once, and all too sudden.

"You must save your family, Leaf," Mantru urged his friend. "Don't delay. Go now!" He patted Leaf's head, gave him a thin smile, and at once slid down the trunk with his heels dug into the deep furrows of the bark. "Goodbye, Leaf! Find me when it's all over and we'll have tea again!"

Leaf watched Mantru hop from the trunk to the ground. He heard sad, mumbled goodbyes, and saw the old Twig hug the twins and pat Fern's head. Then, with baskets full of tearful creatures strapped to the little ridgerunner's back, Mantru stomped off into the forest.

"Bye, bye, Mantru," Buddy and Burba's voices mixed together as they yelled after him. "Bye, Bumper and Winkers and Flip and Poppy and Puff and squeakers." The twins jumped up and down on fat mushrooms to keep sight of Mantru's orange hair and goat-horn cap as long as possible.

Mantru turned once to wave, and shout back, "Twigs are meant to grow!"

Puzzled, Burba and Buddy scratched their heads.

"What's dat mean?" wondered Buddy.

Chapter Eight

SEPARATE PATHS

From the Old Seeder's porch Leaf gazed at the distant gray line of trees marking the Great Gorge. *Will Star be safe? Of course, she will,* he reassured himself. *She's far away from Echo Peak and the Long Ice.* He looked out toward the fork of the Blue Band where Pappo and Mumma were weaving baskets on its banks. *We must all go there right away,* he decided. *The river will take us to safety... away from the Long Ice.*

"Loooook! Loooook!" Shrieks from the twins below startled Leaf so much he nearly fell off the porch. "Hey, Leaf! Look who's here!"

"Who?" Far below, through the thick branches of the old tree, Leaf caught sight of the familiar speckled fur of Speckles and Claws twinkling in the sunlight. Their happy chirps floated up.

Whisper poked her fuzzy ears out of her knothole, and with a chittering of happy surprise she popped out.

Whisper scampered upside-down the trunk to her dear friends. After a few moments of chippie kissing, Speckles nudged Whisper toward the deer path, which wandered in the same direction where Mantru had trekked not too long ago. Claws stuffed a few blossoms in his mouth, unconcerned. Speckles kept pushing Whisper until she whirled around and chattered at him to stop.

Fern shouted up. "Look, Leaf! Speckles and Claws are here! And Speckles is acting strange."

Leaf yelled back. "I see them. Where are Rustle and Feather?" He searched the path and trees nearby but did not spot them.

Buddy yelled, "Dere not here, Leaf. It's just dere chippies, and dere worried."

"How do you know they're worried?" Burba sneered.

"Cause I do," retorted Buddy.

Leaf swung down from branch to branch and landed with a plop on a flat-topped mushroom.

At once, Speckles chattered at Leaf with insistent and demanding chirps. He paused to swallow a fat worm, but then hopped back and forth in front of Leaf, chittering, at once both excited and angry.

"Too bad we don't talk chippie talk," murmured Fern. "Wonder what's wrong with him?"

"Well, maybe they're lost? They probably need help finding Rustle and Feather," decided Leaf. "Hey, Listen, Fern. Mantru was really worried about Echo Peak and the Long Ice. He thinks all the ice is gonna melt soon and slide right off the mountain. He says we need to leave right away and go find Mumma and Pappo." Leaf told her all that Mantru had said, and about the chompers.

Worried, Fern wrung her hands together. She nodded at the end of Leaf's explanation, touched Leaf's arm, and spoke low so the twins would not hear. "If Mantru says it's not safe to stay here then it's not. He would know. Leaf, you need to find Rustle and Feather and tell them to find safety, too. I'll take the twins to the fork in the river."

Leaf glanced at Speckles. He skipped up and down the trail, and tried to push Whisper along with him. "I better go find them right away."

"Yes, don't worry. I'll find Mumma and Pappo. You go." Fern clapped her hands. "Buddy. Burba. We are going to the Blue Band and help Mumma and Pappo weave baskets. Now go up right away make a travel pouch for yourself! Off you go!" She shooed them up the mammoth trunk to their haven. "Don't forget your covies!"

With a rush of unexpected affection Leaf hugged Fern. He realized she hadn't given a thought to the Old Seeder, only the safety of the twins. For once he was grateful for her bossy, selfless attitude.

"Yay!" exclaimed Burba as he scrambled up the Old Seeder as quick as a squirrel who'd stolen seeds from an angry blue-jay.

Buddy paused a little ways up, and called back down, "Where ya going, Leaf?"

"Oh, Speckles and Claws will help me find Rustle and Feather, and we'll catch up with you. Bet we can make it to the fork in the river before you!"

"Betcha' can't, Leaf." Buddy called back. He continued crawling up the mammoth trunk like a slug, careful of his hold on the rough, red bark.

"Goodbye, Leaf," Fern said. "We'll see you at the river then." She hastened up the trunk to stuff whatever she could in the tall baskets they used for traveling and picnics.

Leaf followed Fern up the Old Seeder as far as where his hunting tools were stowed. He dropped the string of the carved whistle-tube over his head, and slung his flaxen rope across his chest. The shoulder strap's pockets were already stuffed with seeds and nuts. Leaf pulled his walking stick out. His saver was beautiful with intricate carvings Pappo had etched. A milky-blue gemstone had been tied into the knothole at its tip. Leaf could not help catching a ray of sun in the stone and scorching a piece of bark with the hot beam. A thin curl of smoke rose up through the branches.

Fern and the twins popped out of the haven with loaded baskets tied over their shoulders and across their chests. They wore fern hats which were perfect to hide beneath should they need to do so. Fern led the troop down the trunk to the forest floor where Leaf stood waiting.

Speckles bounced up and down on the deer path, clicking his annoyance. It was obvious he thought Leaf was taking too long and needed to follow him right away. Whisper and Claws sat in a fern and looked for colorful beetles to munch.

After a quick hug and a whispered exchange, Leaf and Fern waved goodbye to each other.

"We're gonna beat 'cha dere!" Buddy shouted. "We're gonna be dere before you, Leaf!"

Fern, Buddy, and Burba marched off on a narrow, sunlit trail. Burba whistled in time with their steps, but he discovered blowing spit bubbles at Buddy was more fun.

"All right, Speckles," Leaf called out. "Let's go find Rustle and Feather." Leaf trotted to Whisper, patted her nose, hopped on her back, and held on to the thin braid Whisper wore around her neck. Leaf grinned. It was always a good feeling to ride a chippie, and Whisper enjoyed carrying Leaf wherever he wanted to go.

Speckles led the way into the shadows of the fern-covered path created by the gentle steps of soft-eyed deer. Whisper skipped behind him, happy to be with her friends again. Claws, often side-tracked, chased dragonflies off the path, and somersaulted after grasshoppers, but somehow he managed to keep up. The morning sun was warm. Tiny, blue butterflies fluttered around the chippies' ears and rode on their tails.

Leaf leaned over Whisper's neck and gave her a hug. He knew they loved adventure even if it was only finding a couple of lost Twig friends. Leaf wasn't worried. *Rustle and Feather are probably just stuck in an eight-legs web or playing a hiding game with the chippies,* he supposed. *Or maybe it's just a trick to get me to come visit them.* Still, Leaf knew he must find them right away and share Mantru's warning.

As Whisper leapt over a moss-covered log Leaf caught sight of Echo Peak framed by the blue sky. From its tip a wisp of white smoke curled upwards. *Funny. That looks like the same curl of smoke from the bark I burned with my saver*, Leaf thought. *Could smoke be inside the mountain?* Then Leaf grinned at his own silly notion. *What a nuthead. How could Echo Peak be on fire?*

Chapter Nine

LOON

Not far from the sheer drop into the Great Gorge the laughter of six Twig babes floated with the blue butterfly wings flickering in the sunny meadow.

Hemlock crawled through the tall grass to be closer to Star. He was as slow and cautious as a bobcat on an unfamiliar trail. His dark green hair fell to his waist and a few teeny pine cones littered the ground where he had crept. Hemlock didn't worry about losing cones for more always grew back. He only worried about the deep green color of his hair. It threatened to betray him in the light shade of the meadow grass for hemlock fronds blend better with dark, mossy forests.

Snores from the Cappynut twins nearby startled a dragonfly. As more snores erupted the dragonfly rushed away in a flash of brilliant, gossamer purple. Ruffle and Tuffle stirred, awakened by their own struggling snores. They yawned, blinked, stretched, and sat up.

Hemlock paused. He caught a glimpse of the twins through the grass, and frowned. Although they had no skills to track him in the grass, they might stumble upon him by accident. Their silly feathers and constant bickering reminded Hemlock of fledgling crows wailing to be fed. Hemlock tilted his head and listened to the creaking grumbles of PapaMook and the answering grunts of Sapper. Their argument seemed to be about the age Twig sprouts should first hunt.

"Storytime, babes," Star called out.

Hemlock's face brightened. He continued crawling through the grass until he reached a warm hollow nearer to Star where a fawn had slept the night before and left a faint fragrance of milk.

"Listen, now, all of you!" Star's voice drifted like dandelion fluff. "If you are quiet when you rest, PapaMook will tell an especially long story!" The babes scattered at once to their patched covies.

"Tell a story, PapaMook! Tell a long story!"

The tiniest of the Twig babes Breeze left her covie and tugged at PapaMook's sleeve. "Tell us a long, long story," she insisted.

Star waved her back to her pillow. "Shoo!"

"A long story!" whispered Ruffle to Tuffle. "And berries, too, eh?"

Tuffle didn't wait for an invitation to join the story circle or eat berries. He plopped down beside his paps, Sapper, and grabbed a fistful or orange huckleberries. "Stories are always better with berries!" he declared.

"Better with berries! Better with berries!" chanted the babes.

Ruffle elbowed his way between Sapper and Tuffle, and grabbed an even bigger fistful of berries. "Leave some for me!" he muttered to his brother.

"All right, all right, Ruffle and Tuffle." Star waved her hands to quiet everyone. "There are plenty of berries for both of you. You two are worse than the sprouts."

"Not worse than me!" declared Pool. He was the oldest of the babes. He puffed up his chest and crossed his arms. "I'm worse than they are!" Pool looked confused for a moment. Somehow his protest didn't come out the way he intended.

Star gave Pool an amused smile.

Moon nudged him with a wink. "You are definitely worse than they are."

Pool gave Moon a half-hearted grin and nodded in agreement. "Right!"

The Twig babes giggled and whispered back and forth, "Better with berries! Better with berries!"

Star clapped her hands. Now hush everyone so we can hear PapaMook's story. Shhhh!"

With gusto and loud smacks the Cappynut twins continued to slurp berries like greedy bear cubs slurp honeycombs.

Everyone frowned at them and hissed, "*Shhhhhhh!*"

Ruffle and Tuffle gave weak grins to Star, and sucked one berry at a time.

Sapper gave an enormous yawn. He was ready to take his after-meal nap. He'd already heard most of PapaMook's stories, so they always put him to sleep. He snuggled up to a clump of soft dirt.

PapaMook scoffed at him, "You're gonna miss a great story, Sapper." PapaMook winked at Star. "And a scary story, too! A real scary story that's gonna curl Twig toes!"

"Ooooh!" gasped the Twig babes. Their eyes grew large. They became very quiet, unsure whether or not they wanted to hear this story after all. They scrunched closer together.

Star smiled. She stretched out on her side, propped her head up on her hand, and drew in the dirt with a thin stick. Once again, she sketched Echo Peak with the bubble puffing out of its side.

PapaMook crunched up his face until his crinkles resembled the oldest knothole from the oldest trees in the forest. His voice crackled when he spoke.

"Now, listen. Here's the story of one of the oldest and scariest trees in the dark forest.... the Hemlock Twig that got stuck in her tree. She was trapped there forever. At night the whole forest heard her moaning and wailing like this, *OOOYYYOOYEEEEOOYYYHH*"

The sprouts gasped. They rolled themselves into their covies, and pressed together until they looked like a giant, lumpy cocoon. With disdain Pool left them, and sat beside Moon. Ruffle and Tuffle crawled behind the babes, and peeked over the top of the patchwork cocoon. Sapper sat up. He decided his nap could wait.

Nestled into his warm fawn hollow, Hemlock grinned and lay back with his arms crossed under his head. He was surprised PapaMook knew about the oldest Hemlock Twig of all. Even so, his story already sounded made up for the most part. PapaMook didn't even know her name. Hemlock relaxed, gazed at the blue sky, and drifted into a disturbing, drifting memory.

Hemlock Twig sprouts drew stories in the dirt about her, and watched for her blood-red warnings etched on trees to *go no further!* Her name was Loon, and she did not tell stories. Instead, she howled from the darkest hollow in the rainforest. Her eerie wails dripped off the moss-heavy limbs of ancient hemlocks and spruce, and turned back those sprouts foolish enough to answer a dare.

Hemlock remembered when seasons ago he had ventured past the warnings. He was so young.

Older, meaner sprouts poked sticks at him, hissed, and shoved him toward the darkest path in the rainforest. They dared him to search for Loon. So Hemlock entered the murky, tangled groves. He crawled over heaps of soggy moss, crept along gloomy wet paths, and slipped over lichen-cloaked limbs searching for the giant hemlock tree that shrouded Loon's disfigured body. He journeyed deep into the suffocating stillness, and listened for her twisted whispers to guide him closer to the heart of the forest.

At last, a sad murmur disturbed the air. Hemlock followed it to an enormous, ancient tree. He hid behind a moss-covered rock. Hemlock stared at the tree's enormous roots – its twisted knots and whirling bark, and at last it gave shape to the oldest Twig he'd ever seen.

Loon sensed Hemlock hid there. She hissed at him to go away, but he was too terrified to move. Moss dripped from Loon's hands. They curled upon themselves like snakes draw back their heads before striking. Shriveled cones splintered off her head. Burls of rotting bark concealed her eyes. Her face was twisted beyond all recognition of the exquisite stick creature Loon had once been thousands and thousands of seasons ago.

Loon moaned. From deep within the hollow trunk of the hemlock tree a murmuring breeze floated toward Hemlock. Somehow, even without words, he understood her feelings – her song. After a long while, Loon waved her skeleton-like fingers and beckoned Hemlock to come closer. With faltering steps, he did. Loon whispered her wordless story and Hemlock understood.

There had been a time seasons and seasons ago when Hemlock Twigs could speak. A time when Loon could have wandered as other Twigs could free of her tree-home. But unlike other hemlock trees in the forest, hers was different. She sprouted from a hemlock whose heart was twisted and cunning. Its embrace was jealous. It whispered to its young sprout Loon in her dreams, urging her to stay, seducing her with a belief her tree was the most magnificent in the forest – flawless – better than all the others. Loon was deceived, and believed there was nothing to learn or enjoy beyond its own branches. Her heart was imprisoned. And so, she refused to leave her perfect tree-home.

Loon called to other Twigs in her Branch to join her there in her splendid tree, but they were busy with curious wanderings, and caring for their natural sprouts. Loon told them they would find wonder and bliss in her tree's branches, but none answered her entreaties. They were wary of the twisted majesty of her hemlock tree. Loon grew sad for no other Twigs ever visited.

As the seasons passed she climbed up and down less often. She clung to the branches during storms, ate the seeds which blew onto the limbs, and drank from pools in the moss. Confused and sad, Loon still believed there was no reason for her to leave and that her tree was perfect. She stopped calling out to other Hemlock Twigs when they passed by, and soon they forgot she lived there.

Loon hid in her tree, and stared at the world around her. She moved less and less. One day she realized her legs had become stuck in the trunk. Her back had shriveled into the furrows of the bark. Loon struggled to free herself, but soon realized she would be stuck in the hemlock's trunk as long as the tree lived... and hemlock trees were eternal. Her chance to walk the forest paths was gone forever. She would never learn anything new or see anything beyond the heavy branches of the tree. Loon bowed her head and accepted her fate.

Still, the murmurs of living creatures offered her a secret friendship. Old trees in the rainforest whispered to her. Wayward winds brought her stories and comfort. She lost her desire to speak as Twigs speak since those who passed by never spoke to her. Instead she shared rumors with the forest.

It was then Loon witnessed the most absolute terror of all.

One violent day the earth shook the forest with a force mightier than the worst of storms. Land waves rolled from Echo Peak and toppled one tree after another with horrifying, random cruelty. Earthquakes from below the mighty mountain lay siege to all life near it. Heavy branches split from their trunks and fell, smashing everything below in an instant. Creatures abandoned the heaving forest, but trees had no choice but to remain at the mercy of what was to come.

Loon's tree was her refuge. She pressed even deeper within the trunk. After days and days of restless land waves it took only one more to split the mountain open. Unrestrained at last Echo Peak exploded. A boiling tower of ash blasted the shimmering peak to pieces. In an instant the rainforest was burnt and choked by smoldering ash. Only the smoking, ragged-edges of the blasted peak stirred in its own nightmare.

Loon's hemlock tree was scorched beyond all recognition. But it did not die. Deep within its trunk Loon survived to witness life returning to Echo Peak. Small, furry creatures dug their way up from deep burrows where they had hidden from the fiery ash. Slender, green sprouts pushed up through the heavy sludge, and reached for the sun. Creatures returned – marmots, beavers, elk, eagles, deer, and more. Rain washed the flattened logs. Streams cut through the ash. After a long while trees covered the land again like a green sea and velvet moss turned the forest floor lush. Even Echo Peak became a glistening-white cone once more, sheared by rain and wind, and soothed by vast, deep glaciers, which thickened as seasons passed.

Season after season Loon waited, but Twigs did not come back. Eventually, her own hemlock tree sprouted Twigs and the Branch of Hemlock Twigs lived again in the forest. But like the hemlock tree from which they sprouted, they nurtured their twisted jealousy. Like Loon, they never spoke. They skulked away from her to live in moss-enshrouded knotholes, and abandoned the hemlock tree which had nurtured them. In the darkest of nights the forest echoed with their tantrums and rages. Once more Loon was left alone.

Loon wept this story to Hemlock. Her anguished wails made him weak with sorrow. She had been ensnared by the vicious lies of the very hemlock tree that sprouted her. For once Hemlock was glad he could not speak for he had no words to comfort her anyway. After a while he realized his limbs had grown heavy... so heavy he was afraid he'd never move his legs again. Her grief entrapped him. Hemlock struggled to free himself. Loon howled at him to stay. Afraid he'd be rooted there forever Hemlock grasped hold of the low-hanging moss, and pulled and pulled until his feet broke free. He ran away as her furious shrieks pursued him.

In the meadow, deep in his dream, Hemlock lay in the fawn hollow and kicked the clover. In his nightmare he ran through the forest as Loon's wails chased him on dark paths. He moaned and fought the heavy stalks of grass above him. In the strange way dreams jump about, he was suddenly swept into a ferocious, violent, storm. He choked on splintered, glassy ash and shrank before crackling lightning from a violent, churning black funnel above Echo Peak. He was sucked into the swirling storm. Panicked, he struggled to save himself.

In the instant a heart skips a beat Loon's wails pierced Hemlock's fear, and her meaning was clear. *Who believes a mountain explodes?* she howled over and over. *Who will believe?*

Paralyzed in his dream, Hemlock lay still.

Star's soft voice floated into Hemlock's nightmare, and urged him to awaken. "Hey there, young Twig. Wake up. You're only dreaming. It's only bad sleep stories. Come on, now, friend. Wake up." She shook his arm.

Hemlock sat straight up, snapped awake by Star's touch. He stared at the silver-haired Twig staring back at him. Her leafy head blocked the sunlight from his eyes, and he blinked at the glowing halo surrounding her head. More leafy-headed Twigs encircled him. Then he saw the Cappynut twins' silhouettes.

At once he sprang up. The Twig babes giggled, and crowded around him, leaving him no path to escape. He searched for an opening through the tiny Twig bodies pressing against his legs, but was trapped. Hemlock looked with wary eyes from one Twig to another. He was shocked he had been discovered asleep and defenseless. One hand gripped his rope as he held up the other, warning the ring of Twigs to keep their distance.

Pool poked him with a stick. "You awake now?" he asked. "Did ja' have sleepy scares?"

All the Twig babes nodded sympathetically. They knew about sleepy scares.

Star took a step closer to Hemlock. "Don't worry. You're safe. We won't hurt you." She slid her warm hand over his outstretched one, and pulled him toward their picnic baskets.

Hemlock glanced over his shoulder, and scanned the meadow's edge, wondering if other Hemlock Twigs watched. His eyes met Star's.

"Please join us. You are welcome," she soothed him. Star waved the others away. "Go away now, all of you! Can't you see he's shy?"

Reluctant to leave, the babes wandered off, but not too far. They pretended to be fascinated by the fluffy tips of dandelions, and remained close enough to listen. PapaMook, Sapper, and Moon sat on a fallen log nearby. The Cappynuts stole one of the picnic baskets, and dumped it out on a blanket. Having lost interest right away in the strange Twig and Star, they sorted through the treats for the biggest berries and nuts.

Hemlock knew he should run away. He shouldn't be here...with these Twigs, but he felt Star's gentle tug, and heard her kind words, and so he allowed her to pull him down onto a mossy pillow. Once again, he searched the shadows in the trees surrounding the meadow. *What will the others do, if they see me here?*

Star kept her hand tight around Hemlock's and sat beside him. Once again she waved at the Twig babes to go away. Exasperated, she asked Moon, "Won't you please make them go play in the water, or something?" She patted Hemlock's hand and gave him a reassuring smile.

With stern insistence, Moon shooed the babes to the creek. He pushed PapaMook, Sapper, and the Cappynuts away. Once he'd organized the others on the stream's embankment, Moon returned and stood near Star, just in case. He studied the strange Twig with narrowed eyes, and lightly tapped the sharpened rock shard he kept tucked in his belt.

Unsure what Moon intended, Hemlock glowered at him.

Star glanced at Moon, and shrugged. "Don't worry, friend. Moon's my brother. You can trust him." She frowned at Moon. "Be nice."

Hemlock looked down at Star's hand holding his. After a while he glanced up, and gave her a slight smile.

"Now there, friend," Star chirped with a bright smile, "What's your name?"

CHAPTER TEN

THE WARNING

Hemlock's dream still clung to him. *It felt so real!* He shivered with the memory of his desperate struggle in the ash cloud. *Is Loon's story real? Do mountains explode?*

"What is it?" Star asked, concerned by this strange Twig's sudden, troubled expression. She patted his hand.

Hemlock's dark green eyes met Star's. *Loon's shrieks were a warning,* he felt certain, *but about what? Land waves... land waves.* The next moment he knew what he must do. *Somehow Star must be warned if land waves happen here, then Echo Peak will explode. She must know this.*

"It's all right," Star spoke gently. "Don't be afraid. You're safe here." She noticed him staring at the drawing of Echo Peak and the bubble she had sketched in the dirt earlier. "Do you like to draw? Here, go ahead." Star handed him a stick.

Hesitant at first, Hemlock held the stick above the earth. *How do I draw land waves?* He drew a straight line, frowned, and then brushed the line away. He thought for a moment, and then drew a long, wavy line.

"Hmmm," murmured Star. She studied his line. "Hmmm..." Her finger tapped her chin.

Moon glanced at Hemlock. His fingers still tapped the rock shard in his belt, but curious, he peered over Star's shoulder at Hemlock's line in the dirt. "What's he doing?" he asked.

"He's trying to tell us something," she stated, and then whispered over her shoulder, "I don't think he can talk."

"Well, I bet he can still hear," replied Moon. In a loud voice he said, "What 'cha doing?"

Worried, Hemlock glanced up at Moon. He frowned at his wavy line. Frustrated, he brushed it away. He pointed to Star's drawing of Echo Peak. Then he drew peaks to the west of the huge mountain and rolling circles to the east.

"Yes, yes, those are the Sharp Peaks and those are the Blue Mountains, right?" Star asked.

Hemlock nodded and smiled.

Star picked up another stick, and drew two parallel lines. "And here's the Great Gorge, eh?"

Again, Hemlock nodded.

Star drew a circle just south of the gorge lines. "And here we are, yes?"

Hemlock stared at the drawing in the dirt for a moment. He scratched out a long, wavy line from edge of Echo Peak to Star's toes. He reached over and shook her foot.

"Hey!" Star cried out, and yanked her foot back.

"Watch it," warned Moon. He clutched the sharp shard in his belt tighter.

Hemlock scowled at Moon. He drew another long, wavy line to Moon's toe, and grabbed his foot.

Moon scrambled backwards. "Hey, watch it! My foot's mine!" He glared at Hemlock.

"Look, Moon. Look at these lines he drew. Do you think he means land waves?" Star wondered. She asked Hemlock, "Are these land waves... like when the ground rocks?" She swayed back and forth with her arms outspread as if she were trying to keep her balance.

At once Hemlock grinned and nodded. He drew a wavy line in front of the outline of Echo Peak which Star had drawn, and then another and another and another. With an expectant look Hemlock looked up at Star and Moon. He stabbed at the lines and swayed back and forth.

Star leaned close Hemlock and with an encouraging nod said, "Go on. You want to tell us something about land waves, yes?"

Hemlock pointed at the drawing of Echo Peak. For the first time he noticed the bubble Star had drawn on its side. He tapped it a few times with a thoughtful expression. He looked up at Star, a question in his eyes.

"Yes, yes, I saw a bubble on Echo Peak from the tip of our tree-home." Star answered. She pointed up at a treetop. "The bubble is growing bigger every day." She stretched out her arms.

Hemlock's eyes grew wide with alarm. He grabbed Star's arm, and shook it like a Twig shakes a limb to make cones drop.

Confused, Star pulled her arm away.

"He sure is acting nutty," said Moon. He took a step nearer to Hemlock. "Careful, Twig."

"Moon, he's just trying to tell us something," Star reassured her brother, and waved him away. "So... the bubble on Echo Peak is making the land waves, is that it?"

Agitated now, Hemlock nodded furiously.

Unimpressed, Moon asked, "So what?"

Hemlock stabbed the bubble on Echo Peak like an angry jay stabs a beetle. With fierce slashes he gouged wide spirals rising up from the tip of Echo Peak. The spirals grew wider and wider until the deep furrows into the dirt ran away from the mountain in all directions. He drew trees and then with furious strokes smashed them. He drew stick figures and with one sweep of his hand obliterated them all. At last, Hemlock sat back on his heels. His face was dark and grim. With a deep sigh he surveyed the mess he'd made. There was nothing left of the sketch except the Sharp Peaks, the Blue Mountains, and the gorge. He looked from Star to Moon, desperate for them to understand.

Moon stood as still and as silent as a rabbit will freeze when hunted by a fox. His eyes were locked on the frenzied scratches in the dirt.

Star looked shocked. "Moon," she whispered. "Moon, this is the same story PapaMook just told us about Echo Peak. About when it exploded long ago... about land waves and its bubble bursting. Only, only..." her voice faded into a weak murmur. "I think it must be happening again... now. I don't think this is just a story."

She touched Hemlock's hand. "Are you saying we're in danger?"

Hemlock leapt to his feet, grabbed Star's arm, and dragged her toward a deer path which led to the Great Gorge. He pointed at Echo Peak and then at the path. He waved his arms at the Twig babes, Sapper, PapaMook, and even the Cappynut twins, and motioned they should all go with him on the deer path to the Great Gorge.

Star whirled around to Moon, and cried out, "Moon! He wants us to go with him and hide! He's trying to protect us!"

Hemlock took a few more steps toward the path. He returned to Star, gently held her hand, and urged her to go with him down the path.

"You know a place where we can be safe, right?" Star asked with a hopeful tone in her voice.

With solemn eyes, Hemlock nodded. *Yes!*

"Star," Moon's voice sounded faint as if he were far away, "Star, if we're in danger, so is Fern."

"Oh, no!" Star gasped, "And Leaf! And Pappo and Mumma and Buddy, and Burba! All of them! Oh, Moon, how can we warn them?"

"Pesky!" Star and Moon shouted his name at the same time.

At once Moon sprinted to the starling, who was hopping nearby in the deep grass, and wrestling a large, green grasshopper. "Pesky!" he yelled as he ran toward the tooler.

Startled by Moon's shout, Pesky hopped backwards, and glared at him, warning Moon to keep his distance. In his beak a grasshopper squirmed and fought for its life. Pesky slammed it on a stone, knocked it out cold, and gulped it down.

Moon slid to a stop beside him. "Pesky, please take me to the Old Seeder... now!" Moon picked up a small, squiggling beetle to entice him. He tossed it in the air.

Pesky snatched the beetle, and gobbled it up. Moon leapt on his back right away. Pesky whistled a sharp protest, hopped sideways, and furiously beat his wings.

Over Pesky's noisy complaints, Moon shouted to be heard, "Star, you and that Hemlock Twig must take everyone to the gorge. He knows a place to hide, I'm sure." He waved at Echo Peak. "Until it's safe. Until whatever happens happens." He nodded at Hemlock. "Thank you, friend. Star, don't worry. Just stay hidden. Pesky and I will find you after I warn Leaf and Fern and their family."

Pesky skidded sideways, and tried to toss Moon off. When that didn't work, he stabbed at Moon's feet, which were stuck under his wings.

"Pesky!" Moon shouted at him. "Stop! We must go to the Old Seeder." Moon grabbed a fistful of feathers, and the braided rope the tooler always wore around his neck.

For the first time Hemlock relaxed. He waved to Moon as if to say, *good luck and fare well, friend.*

At last Pesky grasped the idea he was supposed to fly to the Old Seeder and find Leaf. He began running across the field with huge, awkward leaps. He hopped higher and higher, until finally, with outstretched wings, he gained enough height to jump into the sky with a Twig on his back. The starling circled the meadow to soar higher

"Star, keep that Twig with you," Moon' voice rolled off Pesky's tail. "You'll need his help... until I get back."

Star ran in circles below Pesky, and shouted at Moon, "But what do I do if Echo Peak explodes?"

"Go that way!" Moon yelled, and pointed west. "Go wherever the Canyon River flows! West! To the Red Forest!" Moon's voice faded into the flapping of Pesky's wings. "I'll find you!"

Pesky finally soared higher into the crystal blue sky, and was lost in the twinkling sunrays.

Star stood in the meadow, cupped her hands around her mouth, and yelled at the top of her voice, although Moon was too far away now to hear her, "Tell Leaf... tell Leaf..." Star's voice grew faint as she choked on her words. *I don't know what to tell Leaf,* she realized.

The Twig babes sat in the creek, and watched Pesky fly away. They had covered each other with mud, and now their little, pink mouths were all that could be seen beneath the muddy masks. They chanted with delight, "Moon and Pesky flew away, flew away, flew away! Moon and Pesky flew away, eh, eh, eh!"

On weak, creaky legs PapaMook stood up, and ambled across the meadow until he stood before Hemlock. With a wise, knowing expression he looked from Hemlock to Star and back again.

"So then, Twig," PapaMook asked with an unflustered wink, "the bubble's gonna burst, eh? We gotta leave our home and go to the Red Forest now, eh?"

Hemlock hesitated, and then winked back.

Chapter Eleven

THE CLIFF CAVE

Star watched Pesky's silhouette disappear in the sunlight. "Bye, Moon," she whispered. "Farewell."

Impatient to leave the sunny meadow, Hemlock clapped his hands to get Star's attention.

Star waved at him. "Wait, friend. We must get the others." She sprinted to the creek, and gathered Sapper, Ruffle, and Tuffle around her. She explained to the older Twigs why they must all follow Hemlock to the gorge and hide. Every once in a while, a head would pop up from the huddle, and look toward Echo Peak or Hemlock. After much mumbling and further explanation, Star stepped from the cluster of Twigs and clapped her hands at the Twig babes.

"We're off on a little wandering, dear ones," Star called to them. "Wash off the mud, now, and fill your moss bags full of treats and your cappynut shells full of water. We're following our new Twig friend on an adventure. We're going to find a wonderful new place to play hide away! Hurry up, now. All of you! That means stickytoes and looksalots, too!" She stared pointedly at the lounging stickytoes and looksalots.

The three salamanders, Click, Chirp, and Crunch, splashed out of the water, scampered over to Star, and squatted with their bellies pressed against the grass. Their moist orange-spotted skin gleamed in the sun. Each snatched dragonflies with their long pink tongues, so that now bright blue tails hung from the stickytoes' mouths. They munched and waited for Star to tell them what to do.

"You must be our stickytoes guards once more, dear ones," Star murmured, and tickled each one underneath their chins. They gave her huge pink grins in return.

Veil and Sky uncurled their overlong tails, and with measured, deliberate, two-toed grips on each stem within reach, they descended from the vine-maple tree. Once they reached the ground their scaly skin changed color from blue-green to shades of grassy green and brownish dirt..

Startled by the odd-looking creatures, Hemlock realized right away that hurrying was not something looksalots do.

Star turned to the Ruffle and Tuffle. They straightened up and stuck their noses in the air, ready for action. They knew Star always gave them the most important jobs.

"Ruffle and Tuffle, please find two forked branches, and make sleds for the looksalot. Will you be able to drag them as far as the gorge?"

"Don't worry, Star," Ruffle stepped in front of his brother. "I can pull 'em both. I'm much stronger than him." He jerked his head at his brother, and sneered at Tuffle.

"*I'll* drag 'em both," protested Tuffle. He pushed Ruffle away. "I'm the strongest one!"

Ruffle shoved Tuffle aside, and puffed up his chest. "No, you won't. You can't even pull a Twig sprout!"

The twins wrestled each other until both fell on the ground. Dust clouds billowed around them.

The Twig babes giggled. "Look at them! They look like crawlies – rollin', dirty crawlies!"

Sapper rolled his eyes, jumped over, and wrenched his sons apart. He yanked them to their feet. With arms outstretched between them, he shouted, "Enough, enough, you two nutheads! Go find some branches and make the sleds. Hurry up!"

"Yes, hurry!" Star urged Ruffle and Tuffle. "Once you find the branches, tie some vines on them for pull-ropes.

Remember, you must be polite when you invite Veil and Sky to climb on them, so use your best manners!"

Sapper pushed Ruffle and Tuffle toward a thicket. "Don't worry, Star. I'll make 'em do it right. Hurry up, you two nutheads!" Sapper knocked the twins' heads together. "The day isn't flowing any slower, you two!"

The Twig babes rushed around filling baskets with treats, and stuffing covies in their belts.

Hemlock stood nearby, pacing back and forth, impatient to leave. Every once in a while he clapped his hands and stomped his feet.

With the extra caution of a fragile, knotted-up Twig, PapaMook hobbled nearer to Hemlock. He studied the younger Twig. After a while, he leaned on his walking stick until his nose almost touched Hemlock's.

"So, what's your name then, strange Twig?" asked PapaMook.

Hemlock stepped backwards, and gave him a blank stare. After a moment he patted the hemlock fronds, which covered his head and were full of teeny pinecones.

"Cone?" quizzed PapaMook. "Your name is Cone? One of our Twig babes already *has* that name. That won't do. What's your *other* name? Your *Branch* name?"

Hemlock frowned at PapaMook, shook his head, and patted the deep green fronds hanging from his head, again.

PapaMook shrugged. "Well, never mind. Friend will do for now." He turned away, and grumbled in a loud voice, "No reason to have a name, anyway."

Hemlock rolled his eyes.

Soon the troop was on its way. It was slow going with the looksalots. They rode off-balanced on the rickety stick-sleds. They rolled their eyes in opposite directions, uneasy and fearful. It didn't help that Ruffle and Tuffle tried to race one another. Once in a while one of the sleds tipped too far to one side so that Veil or Sky had to unfurl their tail and wrap it around a nearby plant to keep from tumbling off. While everyone waited, Star would patiently unwind their tail, and chastise Ruffle and Tuffle to pull the looksalots slower. Since the expedition was traveling more like slugs than Twigs anyway, the babes played hiding games in the tree roots along the way. The stickytoes darted in and out of the ferns beside the trail, and flicked out their tongues to whack the head of any Twig babe who hid too long. In this manner, they followed Hemlock along the deer path to the gorge.

By late afternoon, the troop had reached the Great Gorge. They paused at its rim and gazed in awe at the colors of the cliff walls, which fell in a sickening, sheer drop to the Canyon River far below. The yawning empty space from the south rim to the north was only a temptation for the Cappynut twins. Right away they dropped the looksalots sleds, and yanked out their slingshots to outshoot one another. Ruffle and Tuffle whipped pebbles from their slingers toward the opposite rim with astounding strength and precision. Their skill was such, that many of their stones bounced off the trees on the north rim, and cracked their branches. For once, Ruffle and Tuffle admired and encouraged each other with whoops and hoorahs whenever a sharp *WHACK!* echoed back from the North Forest.

Hemlock was impressed. Sapper offered the young Twig his own slinger, and urged him to try, but with a shy nod, Hemlock turned away.

Star called a warning to the Twig babes. "Don't go near the edge, do you understand? The wind whips up from below, and will pick you right up with it!" The babes nodded with solemn faces.

"Treats!" They shouted in unison.

Star gave them each one berry.

At the end of his patience, Hemlock stamped his foot and clapped his hands. After more treats and with quite a few grumbles the troop started off once more. The trail was too narrow now for the Cappynut twins to race each other. The day was growing warmer, and even the stickytoes tails drooped and sketched wriggles in the dirt. Hemlock led them to an ancient madrone tree teetering at the edge of the gorge. Instead of one thick trunk it had split into two. It looked like a tree on legs, ready to march off at any moment. Its trunk was smooth. Its colors were rich – deep red with orange stripes. One of its wandering branches reached far out over the rim, and hung there in empty space far above the river. The troop of Twigs, stickytoes, and looksalots gathered in its roots.

Without any hesitation Hemlock leapt onto the wandering branch, and walked out halfway to its end. He lifted his rope from his shoulder, tied one end around the branch, and dropped the rest of the rope from the limb. The rope dangled and twisted there, blown about by fitful gusts of wind. Hemlock motioned for Star to join him.

Star stared at him in disbelief. *Am I supposed to walk out there?*

"Don't do it!" whispered Ruffle.

"You'll fall off!" muttered Tuffle. "Don't go!"

Again, Hemlock motioned to Star to join him. His eyes twinkled above the hint of a grin.

He's daring me to go out there, Star realized. *All right, then.* She climbed onto the branch, stretched out one toe, and took a faltering step. She felt dizzy. The gusts of wind whirled around her legs. *Don't look down! Don't look down!*

Hemlock walked over, took Star's hand, and encircled her waist to steady her. With casual assurance he guided her to the rope.

Star relaxed. *He's so calm. He must trust his head and his feet,* she thought.

Hemlock pointed down at the cliff wall falling away beneath the madrone branch. The rope dangled before a crescent-shaped shadow with a narrow ledge jutting out before it.

"Is that a cave?" asked Star. "You want us to hide in that cave?" Star frowned. She remembered another cave where her family hid only a few seasons ago. It was their only shelter deep in the North Forest. Leaf had found them hiding there, and had rescued her family from swarms of barkbiters. *Leaf won't be coming to rescue us from this cave,* Star told herself.

Hemlock knelt down, pointed at the cave, and smiled to encourage her. A swallow fluttered from the cave. Another swooped inside. A moment later more swallows soared out. Their wings tilted to catch the wind rushing up from the canyon floor, and they soared away. Hemlock watched them float on the canyon wind, and grinned at Star.

Well, I'm not a flyer, Star frowned at him. Star studied the branch, the rope, and the cave. The rope was not hanging next to the ledge. It was a few arms lengths away. Star shook her head. *Even if we slide down this rope, how are we supposed to reach the ledge? Jump?*

As if reading her thoughts, Hemlock swung the rope far out over the empty chasm and then back to the ledge. The rope swung back and forth. Once again, his eyes seemed to dare Star to do it.

Dismayed, Star suggested, "You know, the stickytoes and looksalots can carry the Twig babes down the cliff wall to the cave."

Hemlock rolled his eyes. *Fine, fine. Let's get going.*

Just then the earth rolled. Hemlock and Star fell to their knees as the branch whipped them back and forth. Hemlock held fast to Star and the rope. The Twig babes screamed, and clung to the roots of madrone. Great slabs of granite fell away from the cliff walls, and spiraled down to the river below. The massive madrone tree groaned and shifted. Its tip tilted toward the vastness of the Great Gorge. Then with a startling abruptness the quakes stopped.

Hemlock glowered at Star as if she were to blame for the land wave. He pointed at the cluster of Twigs who stared back at them with anxious expressions from the old tree's roots. He stabbed the air in the direction of the cave. *Now!*

"Yes, yes, you're right," agreed Star. "We must get to the cave right away. Now, let's see. The babes are bigger now, so the stickytoes can carry only one at a time." She counted on a finger as she said each name. "Click, Chirp, and Crunch can carry Moss, Breeze, and Sand. Sky can carry Cone, and Veil is big enough to carry Pool and Mist at once. The Cappynut twins and their paps Sapper can slide down the rope by themselves." She paused. A sudden worry clouded her face. She placed her hand on Hemlock's arm. "Can you tie PapaMook to the end of your rope and swing him to the cave? He had brittlebark, you know, and he gets weaker the older he grows. I'll go down first, and you swing him near to me, all right? The others and I will catch him." Star was not sure even this would keep PapaMook safe. She asked, "What do you think, friend?"

Impatient with Star's worries and delays, Hemlock only gripped her hand, and jerked her toward the rim's edge.

Star spoke to the back of his head, "Maybe we should look for another place to hide. Do you really think this is the only place we'll be safe?"

Hemlock glanced back. With a grim expression, he gave her a sharp nod.

As soon as they reached the roots, PapaMook met them with an expectant look and a quivering whisper, "So, Star. What's the plan?"

"There's a cave below us, PapaMook. We must all get there right away," Star answered.

"Are the stickytoes gonna carry us again?" asked Pool. His eyes beamed with excitement.

"Yes, yes! We want to ride the stickytoes upside-down again!" shouted the babes.

Star grinned. "Sure! What a great idea!" She clapped her hands to silence them. "Pool and Mist will ride Veil, and Cone gets to ride on Sky. You other three ride get to ride on the stickytoes. Go find vines for the cradles now. Go sprouts! We need to hurry!"

Sapper peered over the rim of gorge at the rope hanging from the madrone branch. "Are we supposed to slide down that rope then?"

Ruffle and Tuffle looked over Sapper's shoulder, exchanged frightened glances, and gulped.

"Why, sure!" exclaimed Star. "That's no problem for Cappynuts, right? But first you must help make cradles? We need to work fast!"

Sapper and the twins set to work braiding vines. Star fashioned baskets from thick stems to make saddles for the babes. It was not long before the Twig babes were strapped in tight. Click, Chirp, and Crunch crept over the rim nose-first, and with cautious grips, crawled down the cliff face carrying Moss, Breeze, and Sand. They disappeared into the cave. Veil and Sky gave Pool, Mist, and Cone a maddening, slow, rocking ride down the sheer granite wall, but at last they made it to the cave.

Fascinated by these strange creatures, Hemlock leaned over the edge of the cliff, and watched the looksalots' descent. He looked at Star, a question in his eyes.

Star smiled. "I rescued Veil – the big one. I think he was dropped as a babe by a giant white flyer that got lost in the mist. We found the blue one later. We call them looksalots 'cause they're always rolling their eyes around. Funny, eh? They make an odd pair for the forest."

Hemlock blinked to hide his disbelief. *Giant white flyers dropping looksalots?* He motioned to the Cappynuts to follow him out on the branch to where the rope hung.

Sapper, Ruffle, and Tuffle placed their feet sideways on the smooth branch, and took hesitant steps. They flung out their arms, and gasped with each gust of wind. Once to the rope Hemlock knelt, and motioned for each of the Cappynuts to slide down the rope. Sapper went first. Once he hung in front of the cave, Hemlock swung the rope back and forth until Sapper's toes touched the ledge, and he let go of the rope.

With a smug grin, Sapper looked up, and called up to Ruffle and Tuffle, "No problem at all! Come on, you two!" He shoved the sprouts far back away from the cave's entrance. "Out of the way, you buds, or those clumsy twins will land on your head!" The babes giggled at the thought.

With eyes squeezed shut, Ruffle and Tuffle slid down one right after the other. Sapper caught them as they swung near the ledge. He had to pry their fists off the rope, and reassure each one they could now open their eyes.

"PapaMook, stay here in the roots until our friend helps you out to the rope. You go after me," Star instructed him. "He will tie you to the rope and let you down nice and easy. You'll be fine, eh?"

"Don't worry about me, now, little one," PapaMook creaked to Star, and patted her head. You go on." He pushed her onto the branch.

Hemlock stepped over and led her to the rope. He gave her an intent gaze, clenched his fists, and yanked down as if to tell her to hold the rope tight.

Star took a deep breath. Her descent was surprising. *This is fun!* she thought. *As long as I don't look down!* Hemlock swung the rope in wide, slow arcs until she could put a toe on the narrow ledge. Since Ruffle and Tuffle wouldn't go near the cave's entrance, Pool and Sapper reached out to yank her inside.

Star called up to Hemlock. "Be sure PapaMook is holding on tight!"

Hemlock offered a steady arm to PapaMook, and led him out on the madrone branch. Once there, he lifted up the rope, and tied the old Twig tight to the end of the rope. Then with a gentle slip he lowered PapaMook into the empty space.

PapaMook stared up at Hemlock with huge eyes. He tried to pretend a gulping chasm did not exist right below his toes. PapaMook swung around in circles, closer and closer to the cave's entrance.

Star stood on the ledge, and reached far out to grab an arm or foot as PapaMook swung past. Pool gripped her belt and dug in his heels. Sapper held on to Pool by his waist, and each Twig babe grabbed a foot or an arm or a hand in front of them to further anchor Star at the edge of the cave. They all leaned back and forth as PapaMook came closer and closer. At last Star caught hold of a foot, and pulled the old Twig deep into the cave. He sat grinning on the cold rock floor while Star untied him with shaking hands. She walked to the ledge, holding the end of the rope, and looked up.

It was Hemlock's turn. With a gentle flick he pulled the end of the rope from Star's hands. He tied it around his waist, and like a swallow, launched himself into a soaring arc with arms outspread as if he were flying. He flew directly into the cave, and skidded across the rock. With a nonchalant nod to Star he whipped the rope around in a circle. It untied itself from the limb above, fell, and swirled into a neat loop at Hemlock's feet. A slight smile betrayed his pleasure when Ruffle and Tuffle's eyes blinked in admiration.

Star gave Hemlock a tight hug and a kiss on his cheek. "Thank you so much for your help, friend! We'll be safe here, I'm sure." She took a step back, but left her hands on Hemlock's shoulders. "Now, you *must* tell us, friend. What is your name?"

Glowing from Star's kiss, Hemlock searched the cave floor for a way to offer his name. He plucked a soft, green frond, which had just sprouted from his knee the day before. He gave it to Star.

Sapper snapped his fingers. He stated matter-of-factly, "He's a Hemlock Twig from the Hemlock Branch. We should call him Hemlock."

To everyone's surprise, Hemlock gave them a huge grin and vigorous nod.

"Well, Hemlock it is, then," agreed Star.

Pool pushed his way between Hemlock and Star. "So why are we here, Star. Eh?"

Chapter Twelve

FLUFFLES

Speckles – always the most responsible chipmunk – led the always-patient chippie Whisper, an always-distracted chippie Claws, and a usually-day-dreaming Leaf back up the deer trail to find the hardly-ever-gone-missing Rustle and Feather.

The moss-covered deer path was strewn with fallen branches and overturned rocks. Leaf swayed back and forth as Whisper scrambled over limbs ripped from trees by the quakes. He waved to Claws to keep pace with the others instead of eating all the orange-painted blossoms he could find by the side of the trail. Leaf knew a full belly encouraged a chippie to take a nap, especially Claws.

At last the troop reached the end of the path, and emerged from the forest into the sunlight. They paused below a steep, rocky ridge. Above them stumpy trees spotted the ridge here and there. Bright blue flowers decorated the slope. Worried by the lack of cover, the chippies searched the sky for skyhunters – hawks and eagles. Claws dove behind a boulder when the shadow of a cloud floated over them at the same time a pine nut dropped. Less skittish than Claws, Speckles and Whisper sniffed the pine nut to be sure it wasn't dangerous. They chattered at Claws to calm down.

Leaf became impatient. *There aren't any skyhunters! In fact, there are no birds of any kind.* The silence gave Leaf the creeps. It was as if the forest held its breath.

"Let's go, Speckles," Leaf grumbled. "Go find Rustle and Feather. If this is a new game they're playing, it sure is a nutty one."

All at once, Speckles froze. His fuzzy ears stiffened and pointed forward. He stared straight ahead at a long shadow, which fell from a large boulder ahead on the rocky trail. Whisper and Claws squatted motionless behind him, one paw lifted, ready to run.

Leaf leaned low over Whisper's neck, so his silhouette would not be visible. He squinted in the bright light to see what it was Speckles saw.

"What is it?" Leaf whispered.

Speckles lowered his head as if straining to see. Then he hopped toward the boulder with tiny halting pounces.

Once near the shadow, he sat down, and chirped it was safe to follow. Leaf slid off Whisper, and crept forward.

A marmot pup sat in the shade of the boulder, sniffling and wiping its eyes with tiny fuzzy paws. The pup's face was lit by a white furry circle around her chin and nose. Tufts of pale fur on her belly made the brown fur over her shoulders appear darker than it was. Her stubby tail had not even grown long enough yet to wrap around her toes. She blew a pathetic, low whistle as she whimpered.

"Well now, look at that! It's a little burrower babe!" Leaf took a step toward the pup, and gently extended an open hand. "Don't worry, little one. We won't hurt you," he murmured.

A shaft of sunlight twinkled over the rocks, and shrank the shadow so that the marmot pup's fuzzy head glowed like dandelion fluff. Her dark eyes blinked in the midst of a golden halo. She was so tiny even Leaf stood taller than she did.

Leaf could not help grinning. "You're pretty fluffy, little one. I bet you're called Fluffles, eh? That's a perfect name for a fluffy babe like you." He tried to pet her head. Fluffles scooted backwards, but didn't leave. Leaf reached out again to try and calm her fear.

"Now, now, Fluffles, I won't hurt you. You must be lost, eh? Just like everyone else today. Where's your mum?" Leaf soothed the pup until it stopped its distressed, low whistle. "Is she lost, too?"

With sad eyes Fluffles stared at Leaf and the chippies, who crowded around her. Whisper nudged Fluffles' ear with her nose, and licked her cheek. Speckles searched the trail for Fluffles' mum. Claws stared at the pup with crossed-eyes and heartfelt concern.

Uneasy, Leaf wondered if Fluffles' mum were nearby and hurt. He knew even if she were hurt, it might be dangerous to help Fluffles. A burrower mum could be unforgiving and ferocious if she felt she must defend her pup. Leaf listened, but heard no panting or scratching which might give away an injured creature.

Leaf studied the pup. "Well, I can't leave you here all by yourself. I guess we better search for your mum, eh? Speckles, did you see her mum?"

Speckles blinked, and scrunched up his nose. He didn't understand Leaf's words, but he decided it must mean it was time to eat. He yanked a blue flower from its roots, munched a few petals, and then hopped over, and pushed it in Fluffles' face. The babe grabbed it with teeny hands and stuffed the flower in her cheeks.

Speckles blinked happily at Leaf, and tilted his head. *There! I fed it! Is that what you wanted?*

Leaf laughed. "Well, that's a good idea, too, Speckles."

Claws and Whisper scampered around collecting blossoms, and tossing them at Fluffles' feet. She perked up right away.

Leaf searched back and forth along the trail, and mumbled while he walked. He noticed scattered pebbles where the pup had emerged onto the trail. Moist paw prints decorated flat stones. "Well, she can't have been here very long. Her tracks aren't even dry. A stream must be nearby. I suppose Fluffles is lost. Maybe she just played too far from her burrow."

Speckles ears twitched back and forth as he watched Leaf walk in circles. He wondered what his words meant, but Leaf seemed to be talking more to the rocks than to him, so he shrugged and returned to munching on blossoms.

"Burrower dens are in the ground in sunny places with lots of other burrower dens," Leaf muttered. "So, we need to search for a bunch of dirt balls on a hill... or in a meadow ... like that one!"

Down the trail from the ridge a soft meadow lay ringed by aspen and birch trees. A sparking stream fell from the ridge, ran alongside the sea of grass and flowers, and disappeared into the forest.

Leaf pointed at the meadow below and nodded to Speckles. "There! Fluffles must live there!"

Speckles looked at him with a blank expression.

"All right, then. Let's go find Fluffles' mum," Leaf called out. He waved to Whisper and Claws to follow, and plunged down the gravel-strewn hillside. Speckles and Claws slid down after him. Whisper nudged Fluffles as if to say she should go with the others. Reluctant to leave her pile of petals, Fluffles shoved them all in her mouth, and then scampered over the rocks down to the meadow.

Leaf followed Fluffles' tiny paw prints into the sparkling water flowing in the stream. It was not long before they emerged on the other side and were lost in the grass.

"See!" exclaimed Leaf. He snapped his fingers and pointed around the clearing. "There are burrower homes all over." Soft mounds of dirt spotted the meadow.

With a sudden rush Fluffles scampered past Leaf, and disappeared into the tall grass. A moment later her frightened whistles pierced the air.

"What is it? What's wrong?" yelled Leaf as he sprinted in the direction of her alarm. The chippies bounded after Leaf. They tumbled over each other in the thick grass until they rolled into the open where Fluffles sat perched on a boulder. One step past, an enormous gash ripped apart the earth. The quakes had sliced open the meadow. Fluffles whistled a mournful song into the dark crevice.

Shocked, Leaf and the chippies gazed at the devastation on each side of the gap. The burrower mounds had been smashed by uprooted birch trees. Clumps of grass hung over the fissure's edge, and hid its abrupt edge, which fell into dark shadows.

The stone on which Fluffles sat teetered over the rim. She blasted a low whistle again. In reply, a soothing, sing-song whistle drifted up. With bright eyes Fluffles nodded to Leaf, and then whistled into the shadows. Her mum sang to her babe again from the dark crack in the earth far below.

"Oh, no," groaned Leaf. He stood beside Fluffles, and peered into the dark. "So your mum's trapped, down there, eh, little Fluffles?" He draped a comforting arm over her shoulders. "For moon's sake, babe, how will we ever get her out?"

Speckles backed away from the gash, frowned, and clucked as if to say, he wasn't going near that dark crack. Claws hid behind a fallen tree. Only Whisper stayed beside Leaf and Fluffles. She studied the shadows below with anxious eyes. Leaf pulled his long walking stick from the strap across his back, stuck it on the rock, and spun the gemstone at the saver's tip until it caught a ray of sun. At once a beam of bluish light burst from the stone, and pierced the gloom in the fissure.

A marmot face with tender, anxious eyes glowing in the blue light of the gemstone gazed up at Fluffles. Fluffles squeaked with joy at the sight. Her mum clucked, whispered chitters, and nodded to the Twig beside her pup.

But at once Leaf felt helpless. He could think of no way to rescue such a large creature. He searched the rubble around the clearing, and hoped for an idea to save the burrower mum. He knew she would never leave the spot where she could see her pup, and Fluffles could not defend herself out in the open like this.

Fluffles' happy expression changed to worry.

"It's all right, Fluffles," Leaf patted her head, trying to reassure her. "We'll find a way to get your mum out of there."

Whisper nuzzled Fluffles and licked her ears.

Fluffles remained on the boulder, and every now and then blew a low, mournful whistle. Her mum whistled back a tune of sadness. Worried, Whisper nudged Fluffles away from the crumbling edge.

Leaf studied the shredded trees beside the crevice. *I must think of something! What would Pappo do? Better yet, what would Rustle do?*

With a sudden, excited chirp Speckles hopped up and down on a thin sapling. Its lay flat with its tip hanging over the edge of the fissure. Speckles drummed his foot on the trunk, and chattered.

"Of course!" cried Leaf. "Good thinking, Speckles! Whisper! Keep Fluffles away from the edge. Claws, where are you?"

Claws peeked above the log where he hid.

"Come on, you nutty chippie," Leaf glowered at him. "We need your help." Leaf shoved his saver beneath the sapling, jumped on to its tip, and bounced up and down with all his strength. Near the roots of the thin tree, Speckles dug his toes in the ground, and butted his head against the trunk. Delighted by his part in the rescue, Claws chewed the roots, tackling the thinnest first. They bounced and pushed and chewed, but the sapling's thickest roots still clung to the ground.

All at once, Whisper and Fluffles joined Speckles and Claws. With a burst of frenzied root chewing and bursting dirt balls the sapling's roots ripped free. The slender tree slid over the edge of the crevice. Leaves flew up and branches snapped, when its tip smashed into the floor of the fissure. Its trunk leaned against the wall like a ladder.

At once the marmot mum scrambled up the sapling in a flurry of bristling fur. Speckles, Claws, and Whisper dove under a pile of rocks. Frightened, Leaf scrambled backwards, fell, and lay tangled up in a clump of matted grass. He froze, hoping to look like a twisted stem from a torn thicket.

The marmot mum leapt from the pit with stiffened legs and chattering teeth. Overjoyed, Fluffles tackled her. The mum licked and sniffed her pup all over until she was satisfied Fluffles was safe. The mum glared at Leaf with suspicion, but decided to hesitate no longer. She shoved Fluffles into the dense grass, and disappeared in the meadow.

Leaf stood up, and shouted after them. "Glad we could help! He dusted himself off, and added, "Bye, Fluffles! Be a good burrower babe!"

Whisper peeked from the rock pile, sighed in relief, and hopped over a log to sit beside Leaf. She looked at him with a question in her eyes.

"Yes, Whisper, I think Fluffles is safe now. We won't see her anymore," Leaf answered her worry. When Whisper's whiskers drooped, he added, "And we won't see her mum, either!"

Whisper glanced over her shoulder to be sure.

Leaf hopped on the boulder, and once again peered into the crevice. "Wonder what's down there? It's pretty dark, eh?" He planted his saver on the rock, and spun the gemstone at its tip again until a blue ray burst from the stone. The streak of light flooded the dark below. Smooth rock walls curved into a long, snaking, black tube. The tube cut through the earth as far as Leaf could see in either direction. Water fell into the tube from the thin creek, which would have joined the stream in the meadow, but was now diverted into the fissure. It splattered on the black rock floor, and created eerie echoes in the tunnel.

Leaf shivered. "Just look at that!" he whispered to the chippies. "A tunnel made out of black rock. Right under our forest all this time, and I never knew! I wonder where it wanders?"

Whisper peeked over Leaf's shoulder, wondered what he had said, and then shrugged. She wandered away to find some worms to eat.

The sun felt hot on Leaf's head. Whisper and Speckles took turns stuffing different colored flowers in their cheeks. He noticed Claws napping in the knothole of a fallen birch. *Taking a nap is a good idea,* he decided. "Rustle and Feather are probably all right, don't you think, Speckles?" Leaf called to him.

Speckles scowled at him. *CHRRRCCIIKKK!*

"What's wrong with you?" Leaf snapped back.

CHRRRCCIIKKK! Speckles scolded Leaf again, and hopped toward the ridge trail.

"All right," Leaf grumbled. "You're right. Come on, then. Let's go. We'll keep looking for Rustle and Feather."

The next instant a *WHOOSH* of hundreds of big-eared bats rose in a furious tornado from the pit. Their wings deafened Leaf. Their scrunched-up faces and curled claws terrified the chippies. Leaf ducked, and covered his head. Whisper crammed herself into a knothole that was already stuffed with Claws and Speckles.

"*AAHHH!*" Leaf screamed. "*AAAAHHH!*"

A weird, strangled sort of noise followed the bats from the tunnel. Horrified, Leaf squeezed under the log below the knothole stuffed with the chippies. He contorted his body to look like a slender branch, and stared with huge eyes at the crevice. Some sort of crazed beasts clawed their way up the sapling. The poor tree's leaves whipped back and forth in a frenzy of swishing branches.

All at once, two dusty, dark figures popped from the gash in the meadow. Feather looked around the clearing, and spotted Leaf cowering beneath the birch. She walked to the tree, leaned over, parted the leaves, and said with a grin, "Oh, there you are, Leaf. I thought I heard you screaming."

"Got anything to eat?" asked Rustle.

CHAPTER THIRTEEN

INTO THE DARK

Pesky and Moon shot through the sky toward the Old Seeder like a stone hurled from a sling-shot. The mammoth tree's silhouette was a stark, green target against the white glaciers of Echo Peak. From such a great height, it was easy for Moon to see the giant bubble on the mountain, which had frightened the strange Twig. The bubble was a mix of earth, gray chunks of ice, and rocks swelling and distorting the side of Echo Peak. Ice sheets slipped off their ancient bedrock like a Twig babe's blankie slides to the floor. Wide swaths of primeval rock lay exposed. Yet, even as desperate as Moon was to reach Fern, he knew he must warn the other Twigs in the forest about the enormous bubble on Echo Peak... that it would burst!

Moon urged Pesky to soar low above the tree tops. He crisscrossed the forest and Wide Valley on their way to the Old Seeder. Gripping Pesky's feathers tight, he ducked under his wings. "Leave the forest, Twigs! Leave!" he shouted. "Echo Peak will burst! You must escape! Warn the others! Leave now! Hurry! Hurry!"

The Twigs in the South Forest were already frightened by the land waves. Now this white-haired Twig yelling from the back of a fierce-looking tooler horrified them. They rushed off in all directions, shouting to others as they fled. Many raced toward the rivers, others toward the gorge, and still others toward the Sharp Peaks or Blue Mountains. Twigs in the Wide Valley simply vanished. They dove into the elaborate prairie dog tunnels and deepest rabbit dens far below the grasslands, hoping the weird Twig on the tooler would just go away.

Moon and Pesky had not yet reached the Old Seeder when, to Moon's surprise, Pesky tilted his wings, and at breakneck speed spiraled down toward a sunny clearing below a ridge. The meadow was ringed by tall, swaying birch trees, but many of them had been uprooted and cast about like stick toys thrown helter-skelter. Moon could see a huge gash running the length of the meadow. Pesky flung out his wings above the grove in a clumsy attempt to brake to a stop. Still, his claws trailed from his belly low enough to rip the leaves off the tree tips as he glided past.

Moon looked between Pesky's leaf-filled claws and caught a glimpse of the astonished faces of Leaf and two other Twigs staring up at him. Nearby three panicked chipmunks dug their way into the earth beneath a log.

Pesky flapped furiously to avoid crashing into a honeysuckle bush, but failed. He and Moon vanished into the thicket. After a moment they both reappeared, one spitting leaves from his mouth with an angry scowl, and the other with a speared beetle hanging from his beak.

Leaf laughed and held out his arms. "Moon! Pesky! What a great surprise! How are you? How's Star?"

Moon grinned. "Well, it didn't take long for you to ask that," he chuckled. "She's fine." A flash of white leafy hair from Moon's head fell forward as he gave Leaf a huge hug. His pale eyes twinkled. "So where's Fern," asked Moon. He looked around the small clearing.

"She's gone with the buds to the fork in the Blue Band to find Pappo and Mumma," Leaf answered.

Moon sighed, disappointed.

Rustle and Feather shot wary glances towards Pesky, who was clawing at stones nearby, and decided to keep Leaf and Moon between them and the weird tooler.

"I've heard of you." Rustle jabbed at Moon's chest. "So you fly, too, eh? Did ja' know I fly?"

"Hallo," chuckled Moon. You must be Rustle. Yes, I fly on a tooler, though, not leaves. I hear you have amazing leaf-flyers, eh?"

With a smug grin, Rustle nodded.

"Hallo, Moon," Feather offered a warm greeting. "I'm Feather. Good to meet you at last. Leaf told us about the terrible barkbiters and the firestorm. I'm sorry you lost your North Forest home."

Moon gave Feather a shy smile, and clasped her hand for a moment. His expression grew serious as he turned to Leaf. "I bring a terrible warning about Echo Peak, Leaf. There is danger coming to your forest, and it's coming soon."

"Yes, a friend already told us," Leaf answered. "He said the ice is sliding down the mountain and we must leave to stay out of its path. I went searching for Rustle and Feather, and now that I found them, we're going to join Pappo and Mumma. Maybe we can float on the Blue Band all the way to Red Forest, and wait there until the land waves and ice slides stop."

Moon frowned and shook his head. "Leaf, there's even more danger than just ice slides. There is a great bubble growing on the side of Echo Peak. It's right above you. There!" Moon pointed at the ridge towering over them. "It's going to burst, and when it does...." Moon's voice faded. "When it does," he continued, "the whole forest will be destroyed... everything... gone."

Shocked, Leaf replied, "So that's why the Long Ice is slipping off the mountain?"

Worried, Rustle and Feather looked from Leaf to Moon and back to Leaf.

Moon continued, "You must go to the Sharp Peaks or find another place to hide right away."

"We shouldn't go to the river?" Leaf asked in disbelief. "We can travel fast... very fast!"

Moon shook Leaf's arm hoping to make him understand. "Leaf, Pesky and I can fly fast, but you will be trapped below the mountain. Don't worry, though. I will find your family, and tell them to leave at once by river. They should not wait for you. It's not safe for any of you to delay!"

Leaf interrupted, "Where are Star and the babes and the others? Are they hiding, too?"

"They are safe," Moon reassured Leaf. "A friend took them to a place to hide. They will follow the Canyon River to the Red Forest, too. We will meet Star there, Leaf."

Leaf stood silent, and then spoke low, "Yes, I guess you're right. There is something is very wrong with Echo Peak, I know it. Even the creatures are fleeing the forest and the mountain. We should leave, too."

Moon whistled for Pesky, who dug up another worm before hopping to Moon's side. "I must go now, Leaf. I must warn your family. Be safe, my friend. I'll see you in the Red Forest." At once he leapt on Pesky's back. "Don't delay!"

With a brisk running start and several awkward flaps of his wings, Pesky lifted Moon up to the sky, and soared in a circle above the birch grove before tilting his wings toward the Blue Mountains.

Rustle frowned as he watched Moon fly away. "I bet we could fly on leaf-flyers to the river, eh? That would get us there fast. See?" Rustle tossed some crushed grass up in the air. It was caught by the steady wind rushing off the mountainside. The grass swirled back in Rustle's face. Rustle spit out the grass, and coughed.

With a sour tone, Feather muttered, "You can't fly that direction unless you want to end up crashing into the cliffs on the Sharp Peaks. Hmm, but you two are good at crashing, aren't you?"

Rustle and Leaf glanced at each other. Once they had flown a giant leaf-flyer high above the Wide Valley, but ended up crashing in a sprawling prairie dog field. Angry poppers had threatened to shred them to splinters, and Feather had saved them.

"No, leaf-flyers are out," stated Feather in a no-nonsense tone. "There's only one way to go – back down into the tunnel. We'll escape like the poppers do. Their deep tunnels keep them safe even through the worst fires. It's the safest place to hide."

Leaf peered over the edge of the crevice into the black shadows. "Well, it must end up somewhere. It looks like it wanders west." He tossed a stone into the pit. "There's probably nothing down there now anyway, 'cause those nightraiders flew away."

"That's right," agreed Feather with a warning glance at Rustle to not say a word. "That's right, Leaf. And I bet this tunnel goes all the way to the Red Forest. So that's the best place to hide, right? Down there."

Rustle mumbled, "It's not like Feather's gonna give us any other choice, eh, Leaf?"

"Oh, don't worry about the nightraiders," Feather assured Leaf with an encouraging tone. "They flew away, for sure."

"Yeah, the other beasts down there are much worse than them anyway," Rustle interrupted.

Aghast, Leaf stared at him.

Feather stepped in front of Rustle, and with a bright expression said, "I'm sure there are beautiful creatures down there, too, Leaf. Lovely creatures that glow in the dark and sing pretty songs and are really sweet!"

Rustle rolled his eyes. "Sure, and maybe there are some that will drag us off screaming and chew us to splinters and stick us in their mud walls."

Feather stamped her foot. "Oh, for moon's sake, Rustle! Let's go!" Feather snapped her fingers, and at once the chippies popped out of the hole they had dug, and skipped to her side.

Before they could take another step, the ground rolled beneath them. The Twigs and chippies rode the small land wave as if they were balancing on a log floating in a river. A moment later it was over.

All of a sudden the honeysuckle thicket rustled and Fluffles and her mum burst from the thick underbrush. Whisper chirped her delight. Fluffles skipped to her, and they touched noses. The marmot mum took hesitant steps closer to the chippies. With wary eyes she studied the Twigs.

"Awww, look at the sweet burrowers! Do you want to come, too?" Feather held out her hand to encourage the marmot mum to come closer.

Leaf grinned. "The little one is Fluffles. The chippies and I rescued her mum from the tunnel down there. We dropped the tree over the edge."

"Great," Rustle exclaimed, and rolled his eyes. "Wonder if we'll have enough to eat now with them along, too."

"Oh, poo," exclaimed Feather. "We'll be fine. Come on, then, sweeties." She motioned to the chippies and burrowers to follow her down the tree into the tunnel. "We're going to explore this wonderful tunnel under the forest. Let's go, little Fluffles. What shall we call your mum, eh? How about Nuzzles?" She called up to Leaf as she climbed down, "Do you think Nuzzles is a good name for Fluffles' mum, Leaf?"

"Sure," Leaf called back. He decided to keep a wary distance from Nuzzles no matter what Feather named her, and stepped aside as the mum nudged her pup down the birch-tree ladder.

Rustle shouted, "You don't want her nuzzlin' you, Feather. You might lose your nose."

"Doubt it," Feather yelled back.

Speckles scampered down the birch ladder, and once at the bottom kissed Feather with a wet nose. Whisper followed next. She cast cautious glances into the dark. Claws hesitated on the rim of the crevice. He trembled. His eyes rolled back and forth from the tunnel to edge of the forest. Worried the chippie might make a dash for the thicket, Rustle shoved him down with his foot. Claws somersaulted through the sapling's branches and landed with a *PLOP!* beside Whisper. She patted his head with a reassuring paw. The three chipmunks examined the black rock with curious sniffs. Satisfied it was just rock after all, they sat and groomed their fuzzy ears and bristling tails. Nuzzles and Fluffles found a smooth hollow in the wall for their own grooming.

Feather called up, "What's wrong, Rustle? Leaf? Come on! The Long Ice isn't sliding any faster!"

"Oh, no," groaned Leaf. He yelled down at Feather, "Pappo says, 'The day isn't flowing any slower', Feather! When will you ever say it right?"

Feather's voice floated up from the shadows. "Oh, come one, you two. Bet I can beat you to the Red Forest!" Her voice echoed from further away. "The tunnel isn't getting any darker!"

Rustle shrugged. "Well, let's go, Leaf."

Leaf watched his friend drop into the gloom. With a sigh he climbed down after him, and stood by the slender birch tree. He gazed up at the circle of light. Leaf knew the forest was no longer safe, but still he hesitated to leave. Whisper nudged him, urging him to follow the others, who were already disappearing into the shadows.

"I'm going," Leaf sighed. He draped an arm over Whisper's shoulders. "Guess we'll be safe here, eh, little chippie?"

"Hurry up, Leaf," yelled Rustle. His echoes bounced off the walls from far down the black tube.

But before Leaf could take one step a rumbling, rolling land wave buckled the ground beneath his feet. The poplar slid from the edge of the tunnel and its limbs smashed Leaf and Whisper flat. Echoing chippie chitters and marmot whistles added to the chaos of cracking rocks.

Then, with a scary abruptness, it was as if Echo Peak exhaled. The ground lay still like the mountain would never breathe again.

Whisper's teeth grabbed hold of Leaf's shoulder strap, and she dragged the him out from under the birch limbs. Leaf draped an arm over her neck, and they ran toward their friends, who were shouting and chittering to them to catch up.

Leaf glanced back once more at the sparkles of sunlight fading from sight, and wondered if he'd ever see the sun again.

Goodbye, forest. Goodbye, Old Seeder.

Chapter Fourteen

SLIPPERS

Pesky dropped from a cloud above the fork in the Blue Band, and trailed his claws in the silver-colored water. He tried to slow his speed with awkward flaps of his wing, but ended up skidding right into the mud on the river bank. Burba and Buddy dove into the cattails to escape the out-of-control tooler. Pesky tugged his claws from the sticky muck, and with an exasperated shrug tossed Moon into the mud.

"Whoa!" exclaimed Pappo with a dumbstruck look on his face. He stood in the shallows of the river beside a bowl-shaped basket woven from cattails and willow stems. He held a hand above his eyes and scanned the sky. "Where did you drop from? Moon, are you still one stick or in pieces?"

"Hallo, Needles and Ivy! Wish you well!" Moon called out a polite greeting to Mumma and Pappo. He yanked a dandelion loose and wiped the mud from his nose, elbows, and knees.

"Welcome!" cried Mumma. She rushed to hug Moon, mud and all. "Wonderful to see you Moon! And Pesky! I'm so happy you're both safe!"

Pesky hopped backwards, and fluffed out his wings, giving every indication if Mumma took a step nearer he'd stab the topknot on her head with particular viciousness. Grumpy and covered in muck, Pesky hopped away to groom each feather. It didn't take him long before he was flipping stones over with his claws. The riverbank beetles had no chance to escape.

With a huge grin Fern padded across the mud bank and hugged Moon. "You're safe! How did you know we're here? How are Star and the Twig babes and PapaMook? What about those nutty Cappynuts?" Fern stepped back, her eyes glowing, unable to hide how she felt.

"Yes, they're all well!" laughed Moon. He could not resist another hug from her. "I saw Leaf. That's how I know you're here. And Rustle and Feather are with him, too." Moon took Fern's hand. "I have to tell you something important."

Pappo waved to Moon, and shouted, "Yes, yes, we already heard that the Long Ice is melting. We know all about it already, ha!" The slow-swirling river currents wrapped around Pappo's knees in confused ripples. With quick stabs of stems and fists he continued to weave the cattails and willows stalks together. The basket took the shape of a shallow raft. "Our old friend, the giant leader of the chompers, swam by early this morning, too, with his whole colony. He was slapping the water so hard we couldn't miss them. We all waved and jumped up and down, too! Guess he figured out the ice slides are comin'!"

"Giant chompers?" asked Moon. Confused, he looked back and forth from Fern to Pappo.

"Don't worry about it," Fern murmured. "Those are the chompers who built the mighty dam above the Old Seeder. They're probably just going on a journey somewhere, and said hallo as they passed."

"Oh," Moon replied, but now his face clouded over, and he looked worried.

Mumma clapped her hands at Burba and Buddy. "All right, you two buds. Wash up and get your covies. Naptime!" To stop their protests she added, "Sapsuckers for both of you, if you're quick!"

Right away, Buddy and Burba splashed a tiny bit of water on their faces, and rolled out their covies.

Mumma dug around in a basket, pulled out two round, sweet sapsuckers, and gave them to the buds. Content, Buddy and Burba watched Pesky stab grasshoppers on the riverbank.

At once serious, Fern asked, "So did Leaf tell you what Mantru said? You never met that nutty, old hermit, did you? Anyway, do you know he told us the Long Ice is melting? That's why Pappo is making big baskets. We're all gonna float down the river to the Red Forest, and wait there until the ice-slides are over. Leaf and Rustle and Feather are coming with us. Will they be here soon, Moon? Are they far behind you? You'll come, too, eh?"

"Fern, for moon's sake, let this young Twig talk!" laughed Mumma.

With a hopeful smile Mumma asked Moon, "So you talked to Leaf? He's on his way to us now, right?" But by the glint in Moon's eyes she already knew the answer to her questions. "He's not coming at all is he?" Her smile faded.

When Mumma's voice faded into a whisper, Pappo stopped weaving. He waded to the river bank. "Leaf is on his way, right?" His voice sounded stern and a bit angry.

Moon's voice was steady. "Needles, please understand. I've come to tell you the ice slides are not the only danger. One side of Echo Peak is swelling up like a huge bubble, and it's going to burst soon. When it does, nothing will be left – nothing from the Sharp Peaks to the Blue Mountains to the gorge and maybe even further. The bubble is so big now it could explode at moment. Leaf is taking another path so he can escape before Echo Peak bursts."

Fern moved close to Moon, and slipped her hand in his.

Moon looked from Mumma's frightened eyes to Pappo's worried ones. "Leaf will find another way to the Red Forest. He says he'll meet you there."

Mumma blinked, trying to hold back her unexpected tears.

Embarrassed, Moon kicked the dirt at his toes. "Um, I'm sorry, but I have to return to the gorge right away. My family might need my help."

Fern clasped Moon's hand tighter. "I'm going with you, then. Star may need my help, too, with all those sprouts and PapaMook so creaky.

Mumma glanced at Pappo, who nodded.

Pappo spoke in a strict voice, almost thinking aloud. "Yes, of course, Fern. You must go with Moon. The chompers took this fork from the Blue Band for a reason. The leader must have been trying to tell us to follow him, so we will float down this fork, too, to the Red Forest. In any case, we will meet you and Leaf in the west. We'll get there somehow." Pappo placed his hands on Moon's shoulders. In a low voice he said, "Please bring Fern back to us."

With a solemn face, Moon nodded.

Fern tiptoed over to the napping Buddy and Burba. She gave each a light kiss, and then returned to stand before Pappo. He gave her a hug and stern instructions, "Use your head, now, blossom. Stay safe and we will see you again soon."

"Be safe," Mumma whispered. She hugged Fern tight, and gave Moon a light kiss on his cheek. "Fare well. We'll see you soon in the Red Forest."

Moon gave a sharp whistle and with a surprising quick skip Pesky was beside him. Moon grasped a few of his neck feathers and leapt on his back. He leaned over and held out his hand to Fern. "Come on, Fern. Don't be afraid."

Pesky tilted his head, and narrowed his eyes at Fern with a suspicious glare.

Uncertain, Fern raised a hesitant hand to Moon.

Moon chuckled, but in a soft voice he reassured her, "Pesky will keep us safe, don't worry, Fern. I'd never let anything happen to you, anyway." He lifted Fern up behind him.

The frogs scattered before Pesky's dash down the river bank. With one last awkward skip and splash through the water, he soared up into a crystal blue sky. His claws left deep imprints in the mud along with a few brush strokes from his wings. Moon and Fern spiraled higher and higher on Pesky's back, up and up into the clouds until Mumma could barely see Fern waving farewell.

Moon's shout drifted down like a feather, "Hurry! Leave now! Don't delay!"

Pappo waded through the shallow water, grabbed the basket-raft he had just finished. He guided it to their belongings, and loaded them aboard. His tone was quiet and urgent. "We must leave, Ivy. Now."

Mumma nodded. "Yes, Needles. Let's go."

Sensing an adventure even in his dreams, Buddy woke up with a start. "So where we goin'?"

Burba sat up. "So is that a river-sled? Are we gonna ride in it?" asked Burba.

"Come on, you two, and remember your covies," Pappo chuckled. He lifted each one into the raft. "Stay there." He bent a cattail into each one's fist. "Hang on to this and don't let go."

"Wheee!" Burba cried.

Buddy peeked over the edge of the basket at the water swirling around them. Frightened, he ducked his head below the rim, and clasped his worn leaf-covie to his chest.

Careful to keep her balance, Mumma climbed aboard. She clung to a fat cattail to steady herself.

"Are we ready?" Pappo asked.

Mumma offered a nervous smile.

Pappo examined the basket one last time for leaks or weak weavings. Cattails stuck out at odd angles here and there, but their stems were bound together as tight as clay.

Burba advised him, "Looks dry in here to me."

"Well, then, let's go," Pappo decided at last. After a strong kick-off from the mud bank Pappo hopped on the basket-raft. "Off we go!"

At that moment a sudden, violent land wave rolled the Blue Band into one large curl over their heads. The grassy banks swayed back and forth, and the basket-raft bobbed high on the river's choppy waves. Excited by the sudden whipping water, Burba shouted while Buddy clung to his cattail tighter. It was over in a moment. Pappo, Mumma, Buddy, and Burba sat dripping and speechless in the raft. After a while the river quieted.

Burba became bored at once with the slower pace. "Are we gonna get there soon?"

"Yeah, when we gonna get dere?" added Buddy. He watched the river with worried eyes.

Nervous, too, Mumma seized two cattails to keep her steady. "Hush, you two. We'll get there when we get there."

"Where is da river goin'?" asked Buddy.

Pappo winked. "The river is going all the way to the Red Forest, Buddy. The chompers are already on their way there. Keep an eye out for them. Leaf and Fern are gonna meet us there, too."

They drifted into swirling eddies, which spun them in circles. Soon the raft was swept into the swift current in the middle of the river.

"Hold on! We're on our way now!" cried Pappo.

Mumma gasped. Her golden, leafy topknot fell over her face. She struggled to right it without losing her hold on the cattails.

"Wheee!" shrieked Burba.

Pappo gave Buddy a reassuring pat on his head.

Soon the raft settled into the rush of the swift-flowing river and the soothing rhythm lulled Burba and Buddy to sleep.

Mumma relaxed her grip, and took a long look behind them at Echo Peak's silhouette. As they drifted further downriver, Mumma began to sniffle and pat her eyes with a soft leaf. Pappo put his arm around her. He wanted to comfort her, but he felt too sad himself to think of any words.

"Have we really lost our home, Needles?" Mumma asked. "Lost the Old Seeder?"

Pappo sighed. "Echo Peak is warning us, Ivy. Warning us that all we know and love is changing. We must listen or we will lose more than our home." He nodded at the twins. "At least we're leaving with our roots. They're safe."

"Do you think the buds understand they may never see the Old Seeder again?" Mumma whispered.

"I don't think so," Pappo murmured. "They won't understand until they've sprouted more memories of their own, and look back instead of always looking ahead to what they want to do."

Mumma nodded. "Yes. Well, Leaf and Fern will miss the Old Seeder. I am so very sad for them. To lose so much before they've even begun to branch out." She sniffled and blinked away her tears.

Pappo patted her hand. "We'll tell them all stories about the Old Seeder and they'll tell their buds and those buds with tell theirs. One day, we'll all live together in another mighty tree." He winked at Mumma. "Of course by then we'll be all knotted up and brittle and squeak a lot, eh, Ivy? And when we're really grizzled we'll sit on old branches again and tell buds our stories."

Mumma sighed, and squeezed Pappo's hand.

A heavy splash near the shore startled Pappo. He spotted an enormous creature plunge into the river, but did not recognize its shape. Its powerful legs pushed through the swift currents to the east bank, where it crawled up, and disappeared into a grove of birch trees. More dark shadows splashed into the river, struggled to cross, and make their way east. Their ghostlike silhouettes melted into the haze of the Blue Mountains.

A steady stream of smaller creatures now slipped into the river. The water became full of black noses, tilted ears, and slapping paws as they swam beside the basket-raft, choosing to be carried along on the river's fast current rather than risk remaining on its shores.

Pappo was reminded of another time when panic-stricken creatures tried to escape a terrifying firestorm. Side-by-side they fled their homes, no longer enemies or afraid of each other, only desperate to survive. Pappo watched these frightened creatures now. They never looked back. Their noses pointed away from Echo Peak. He wondered if they would survive what was coming. *Will we?*

Mumma's voice floated soft and reassuring toward Pappo. "Don't worry, Needles. Leaf and Fern will be safe. And so will we."

The raft bobbed up and down, sometimes swirling in circles, and every so often floated backwards. Pappo rested his chin on his hand, and watched the twins sleeping without care. He grew drowsy, but an uneasy feeling kept him from sleeping. Words kept slipping in and out of his thoughts. He could not quite grasp what they meant. *The Long Ice will slide down Echo Peak... slide down... slide into the lake... the lake will spill into the forest... spill and flood the forest... flood the rivers....*

"Flood the Blue Band," Pappo muttered the words aloud. At once he sat up. He shook Mumma awake. "We must go faster," he whispered.

Startled from her drowsiness, Mumma murmured, "Faster? Aren't we going fast enough?"

"No. We must go faster," Pappo urged her awake. He knelt in the raft and slid the rope off his shoulder. He searched the water around the raft. "I need more rope, Ivy."

Right away Mumma dug into a basket and pulled out another rope. "Here."

Pappo fashioned two lassos and curled them up to his knees. He pointed downriver at a river otter rolling over in the mud on the bank. "Look, a slipper!"

The next moment another otter joined the first. Curious, they watched the Twigs float down the river on the basket made of willows. As the basket drew nearer, they slipped into the water to investigate, and swam directly to the raft. Their black noses, piercing eyes, and silver whiskers floated just above the surface near Pappo.

"Are they going to climb in?" Mumma worried.

"No, I think they're just being nosy," whispered Pappo. "If we rope them, we can go faster."

"Only if they decide not to pull us out of the river!" Mumma cried. "Be careful, Needles."

Pappo whipped both ropes into the air at once. Each lasso dropped neatly over the noses of the otters and tightened around their necks. Pappo dug his heels into the basket, leaned back, and gripped the ropes. "Hang on to the sprouts!" he shouted.

The otters burst into a high speed swim at once. Water blasted past the sides of the raft in curling, foaming arcs. The slippers dove underwater, returned to the surface, and then dove underwater again. They seemed to be having fun.

"Whoaa!" cried Mumma. "Hold on!"

It was as if the raft flew above the river. Two graceful wings of white water curled away from each side of the raft.

Burba and Buddy woke up. Blinking through the spray, the twins gripped the cattails and screamed, "*Yahoooooo!*"

"Swim faster, slippers! Faster!" Pappo shouted. He never looked back.

Chapter Fifteen

ECHO PEAK

It was as if Echo Peak took an enormous breath, and then gasped in disbelief. Leaf felt the tunnel shift beneath his feet and looked down. Rustle and Feather looked up. Whisper, Speckles, and Claws pressed their bellies on the black rock. Nuzzles stuffed Fluffles beneath her.

Then, Echo Peak roared!

Terrified, Leaf, Rustle, and Feather clasped each other tight. The black rock cracked and shrieked their horrific peril. The light was suffocated.

Leaf sank to his knees, reached out for Whisper, and clung to her neck. The faces of his family spun around in his head. He heard a distant, panicked voice screaming, "Mumma! Pappo!"

From a muffled, far-away place Rustle and Feather shouted, "Leaf! Leaf! We have to run! Get up! Hurry!" Feather's voice grew fainter as if she were running away.

"Leaf run!" Rustle dragged him and Whisper a few steps down the tunnel. "Leaf! You must run!"

Leaf tried to stand up, but his legs were shaking.

Whisper bit his foot.

"Ow!" Leaf cried out.

"Good chippie!" Rustle patted her nose. "Come on, Leaf." He pushed him further into the dark tube. They caught up with Feather, who held onto to Speckles.

"Hurry!" Feather urged. Claws, Fluffles, and Nuzzles crowded around her. "Speckles will lead us from here. He's used to tunnels."

They clung to each other, hands to tails. Twigs, chippies, and marmots helped each other stumble through the dark. Last in line, Leaf gripped Whisper's tail. He tried not to think of anything except following the outline of her fuzzy head bobbing up and down before him.

The black rock that shaped the ancient tube beneath the forest held its thick walls against the deep, rumbling explosions of Echo Peak.

Leaf blinked back his tears. *The Old Seeder...*

Chapter Sixteen

ON PESKY

Pesky soared high, but the black cloud rose higher. At first there was no sound. Fern and Moon clung to Pesky's feathers, and looked back in disbelief at the dark, rolling tower of ash billowing up into the blue sky from the shattered tip of Echo Peak. Within the ash storm, lightning surged and flashed like veins set afire.

Fern and Moon gripped each other's hands as if they were afraid the other might fall off the back of the tooler. Desperate to escape, Pesky tilted his wings to embrace a sudden blast of air, which rushed them up and away from Echo Peak.

The eruption churned out blistering ash which rolled over and over down the mountain into the forest. It seared all it touched in an instant. The tip of the Old Seeder – Leaf's lookout – was the first to feel the agonizing blast. In an instant the most magnificent tree in the forest lay flat with thousands of others on a gray deathbed. Their tips pointed in the same direction... away from Echo Peak.

The rainforest with all its jealous hemlock trees where Loon was held captive was the last to be struck. Loon could not see it coming, yet she sensed its cataclysmic approach. At the instant her hemlock tree was set ablaze and uprooted, she was ripped loose from the trunk. With arms outstretched, Loon felt her freedom and smiled. And then she became cinders. Loon drifted away into the Great Gorge.

Moon urged Pesky to fly faster. "Hurry, hurry, Pesky," he shouted. "Hurry to the Great Gorge!"

Terrified, Fern and Moon somehow found the courage to look back. It was as if Echo Peak had shrugged, and its shoulder slipped off its back. What was left of the massive Long Ice glacier slid down the mountainside into the alpine lake, burst through the massive beaver dam, and smashed its way to the Blue Band. The monstrous slurry of battered trees, mud, and boulders rushed downriver, suffocating all life in its path.

The furious tower of ash from Echo Peak rose higher and higher into a shocked, blue sky. An unsympathetic wind carried the ash east and smothered the Blue

Mountains. The stunned Sharp Peaks to the west glowed red. Nothing remained of the South Forest.

Pesky's feathers brought warmth to the two Twigs on his back as the tooler flew high above the stricken landscape. Fern squeezed her eyes shut so she could not see what was left of the South Forest, but one vision remained. *The Old Seeder*. Safe on the back of Pesky, Fern covered her eyes and cried.

The shock to Moon was the same as when he lost his own forest to a horrific firestorm seasons ago. His hidden pain was sliced open, and he cried.

Fern's tears sifted through her fingertips and were whisked into the frigid air by the wind. They fluffed into snowflakes, drifted down into the gorge, and mingled with the floating cinders of Loon.

CHAPTER SEVENTEEN

A CAVE AGAIN

"Pool, help me with the Twig babes," said Star. He had been pestering her to explain why they were all in a cave stuck in the side of a cliff above the Great Gorge. *No need to frighten the babes,* she decided. *They don't need to know.*

Pool stomped away, grumbling something about being treated like a babe again.

Star checked to be sure all the sprouts were safe and unhurt from riding on stickytoes and looksalots. She patted each Twig babe's head, kissed each stickytoes' nose, and stroked each looksalots' curled tail. Then she shook the dust from the silver leaves on her head, and blinked in the dim light.

Ruffle, Tuffle, and Sapper plopped down on the rock floor and shared berries with the sprouts.

"We're all fine," Star whispered to PapaMook. She helped the old Twig to his feet and hugged him. "Well, here we are again... stuck in a cave. Nothing ever changes, eh?"

PapaMook chuckled. "I know what changes!" He slapped his knee with delight as if he had the right answer to a riddle. "Twigs change! Just look at those buds!" The babes were covered in sparkling dust, and giggled at each other's ghost-like, grinning faces.

With a limp leaf, Star wiped the ash off the old Twig's balding head. "Yes, I guess you're right, PapaMook. "The babes change, eh?"

PapaMook patted her hand. "I know a secret, Star." His face crinkled up with an exaggerated wink and sly grin. "When you help Twig babes change, you change, too."

"Yes, yes," Star offered a patient smile and nodded. *Wonder what that means? Poor, poor PapaMook,* she worried. *He's just too old to make sense anymore.*

Hemlock waved to Star to join him in the back of the cave. He pointed at a giant heap of sticks and moss blown against the rock wall.

Star studied the stinking balls of sticks, matted moss, and dead grass. Her voice echoed off the cave walls.

"What are these? They smell rotten." With a grimace of disgust she stepped back holding her nose.

PapaMook appeared at her elbow. "They're just pretty little nests," he answered. "They're nests for the flyers that live here in the cliff. Aren't they beautiful... the flyers, I mean, not the nests."

"Ugh," grunted Star.

PapaMook leaned against the rock wall, and slid down until he sat. Star patted his shoulder, and offered some water from the acorn-flask tied to her belt. The Twig babes scurried back and forth in the dim light. They dragged the bird nests across the cave, and peeked into the narrow holes at the tips of the woven balls. Pool shoved one so hard it rolled right over Breeze and Sand.

"Ow! Stop it, Pool!" they cried, feigning injury.

"Here's comes another!" shouted Pool with glee. With a mighty push, he aimed one of the nests directly at Mist. PapaMook reached over and pulled her out of the way. The nest bounced off the wall, and skidded into the dark shadows at the far back of the cave. Then, to everyone's astonishment, it vanished.

Always the most curious of the stickytoes, Click scurried across the ceiling to investigate, and scampered down the wall. To Star's amazement he disappeared, too. At once Crunch and Chirp darted over. Each crawled down the rock wall and kept right on crawling until they were out of sight.

Veil and Sky began a slow rocking journey toward the back, but before they could make it to the vanishing spot the stickytoes reappeared, clicking and chirping with excitement.

Hemlock rushed ahead of Star and the curious group of Twig babes. He motioned them back. With one last cautious step he leaned forward, and peered down. A round tube, which had been cut into the cave floor long ago by rushing rainwater, fell away at his toes. The loud splashes from the river below echoed up the chute. He looked at Star, pointed down, grinned, and winked.

Star frowned as she joined him with cautious steps. "Even if we made it down, we'd all drown in the river," she answered his grin. "No, we'll just have to climb back up the way we came... once the danger's over, of course." She turned away, clapped her hands, and waved the babes away from the treacherous chute. "All of you stay away from here now. You might fall. Now, it's time for sapsuckers and a long nap."

The babes looked at each other, not knowing whether to be delighted for sapsuckers or complain about a nap.

Then, it came. *BOOM! BOOM! BOOM!*

It was as if gigantic feet stomped across the rocks above them. The Twigs and creatures looked up. Star stumbled to the babes and pulled them into a huddle around PapaMook. In a swift scramble, the Cappynuts dove behind them. Star covered her ears as if she might be crushed by the sound alone, and stared out of the cave's doorway. Across the chasm from the narrow ledge the cliff walls seemed to be shivering. In a protective stance, the stickytoes encircled the Twigs, nose to tail. The looksalots gripped the rocks above them like a scaly blanket.

Only Hemlock acted. In one swift movement he gathered the birds' nests and threw them on top of the huddle. Ruffle and Tuffle struggled to push away the smelly clumps, but Hemlock piled them back on top.

"What is it?" cried Star. "What's wrong?"

Just then, the rocks screamed like a massive fist squeezed the cave. A dark cloud blocked all light. Thick, gray dust billowed into and past the cave's entrance, and then plunged into the gorge. Trees set ablaze swirled through the air.

Star watched in disbelief, and then horror. *Is this it? Did the bubble burst?*

The giant madrone was the last to surrender to the shock of Echo Peak's blast. Scorched and blackened it hung by one desperate root, and dangled before the cave, and then it dropped.

There's no way back, Star realized at once. *We're trapped in a cave again.*

CHAPTER EIGHTEEN

NESTS

In a few moments the thick ash stopped falling past the cave's entrance. The Twigs crawled out of the huddle, and stood up on shaky legs. Star fussed over the babes and PapaMook until she was satisfied all were unhurt. The Cappynuts tiptoed to the narrow ledge to see what they could, but there was nothing except gray ash dripping from the rim of the Great Gorge.

Hemlock pulled Star over to the chute at the back of the cave. He rolled a small nest over the edge. They both watched as it fell far down and splashed into the river far below. It bobbed up and down, and then floated away. The others crowded around.

"The nests!" Star exclaimed. "That's what you were trying to tell me. We can drop down to the river in the nests and float to the Red Forest!" Star laid a hand on Hemlock's arm, and whispered, "But once we make it to the river, there's nothing to stop us from floating apart and being lost."

Hemlock knelt and drew crisscrossed lines in the dust on the cave floor. Then he pointed to his rope.

"Yes, I suppose you're right," admitted Star. "If you can make a net to hold all the nests, we would stay together."

Without any hesitation, Hemlock dragged a nest to the edge of the chute, crawled in it, and rolled himself over the edge. He disappeared in the chute.

Star gasped, "Oh, no!"

They all peered over the edge.

Hemlock's nest bounced off the granite walls and lodged in a crevice just at the river's edge. He stuck his head out of the nest, looked up, and with a grin, waved.

"Thank the moon," Star exclaimed. She waved back, and cupped her hands around her mouth to be sure she could be heard over the splashing river. "Wave when you're ready for us!"

Hemlock nodded. He set to work weaving a strong net from rock to rock.

Ruffle and Tuffle exchanged worried glances. Sapper stepped between them, studied the turbulent river, frowned, and scratched his chin. "Don't know, Star. That's quite a drop."

"It'll be just like flying," PapaMook's voice creaked. "Only it'll be straight down instead of up! We'll float on the river instead of on clouds!"

"Yes, that's it," nodded Star. "The stickytoes and looksalots can crawl down first." She shooed Click, Chirp, and Crunch to the chute. "Go on now you three. Find a good rock to perch on down there, and you catch the babes if their nest misses the net, eh?"

Click, Chirp, and Crunch clung to the cave walls. They licked their eyes and blinked. Water was always welcome for stickytoes, and so they were eager to descend. The stickytoes gave Star a wide pink grin, licked their noses and eyes, once more, and scurried down the walls to join Hemlock.

Star hugged Veil and patted Sky's nose. "You two get started. Once you're down, we'll follow."

Veil and Sky rolled their eyes to remind Star that looksalots don't swim.

Star urged Veil and Sky on with a kiss and a whisper, "You can ride on our nests, can't you, eh? You have very strong grips, you know. We'll keep you dry."

Veil rolled his eyes and nodded. The two chameleons took slow, bobbing steps to the chute, and once there tilted headfirst over the edge, balanced for a moment, unfurled their long tails, and began their descent.

"Here, babes!" cried Pool. Eager to show he was the older Twig babe, he organized the nests, smaller to larger. "You can each have you own nest." Pool lined up the babes in front of a nest about their same size. He shoved one Twig babe after another in their nest, ignoring their protests. "Just hold your nose, if you don't like the smell," he ordered.

Star followed behind Pool and handed each babe a sapsucker. "Hold tight now. Keep your head tucked inside your nest. Hemlock will catch you in the net, don't worry." One little head after another tucked itself deep inside its nest. The sound of slurping sapsuckers distracted the nervous Cappynuts, who held out a hand for theirs.

Ruffle and Tuffle lifted PapaMook into a fat, oval nest. They stuffed in so many feathers for extra padding PapaMook's head looked like it grew feathers instead of leaves. The Cappynut twins wrestled over the larger nests, until Sapper decided for them. With groans of disgust Ruffle, Tuffle, and Sapper climbed inside their nest.

Star stood at the edge of the chute. She waved to Hemlock below. "Are you ready?"

Hemlock's rope web stretched between slivers of cracked granite and a couple of boulders sticking up from the water. He walked back and forth on the rope, and bounced to test it. He signaled to Star the web was ready.

"All right! They're coming!" Star hollered.

One by one Star rolled the nests over the edge, pausing between each drop until Hemlock had rolled the nest to one side or the other. Star was last. She held her breath and her nose, and squeezed inside a small round nest. She closed her eyes, and rocked back and forth until she teetered just at the edge. Then with one more rock she dropped down the chute. The next moment, she felt herself bouncing up and down on the rope web.

Hemlock steadied her nest, peeked inside, and winked. Right away he stuck all the nests into squares he'd fashioned in the rope-web. The Twig babes and Cappynuts poked their heads out of the nests, and grinned at Star.

Star laughed. "So, Hemlock, you made a raft for us at the same time you made a web, eh?"

Hemlock winked. He motioned to the stickytoes and looksalots to stand on the raft.

"We're in a nest-raft!" exclaimed Ruffle.

Tuffle answered in a disagreeable voice, "No, it's more like raft-nest."

"But it's made of rope, so it's actually a rope-nest-raft," countered Ruffle.

"Enough," cried Sapper to his sons. "It's a raft!"

Ruffle mumbled, "It's a nest-raft."

Splashes slapped the bottoms of the nests, and reminded them they were just a toe-touch from the water. They would be swept away as soon as Hemlock dropped the raft into the river.

"Everyone ready?" asked Star. She counted noses. *Breeze, Moss, Sand, Mist, Pool, Cone, Crunch, Chirp, Click, Veil, Sky, Ruffle, Tuffle, Sapper, Hemlock... and... and...* Star searched the baskets, anxious to see the gray, wispy feathers on PapaMook's head. At last he peeked above the rim of his nest. *... and PapaMook.* "Let's go, then!" she nodded to Hemlock. "Hold on tight!" Star shouted, and squeezed her eyes shut.

With that, Hemlock loosened the ropes from the boulders, and jumped into his own nest just as the raft dropped into the swirling river. The raft spun around and around until at last it rode high on the tips of white-capped waves.

Hemlock perched on the rim of his nest at the front of the raft, his eyes fixed on the river's path ahead.

"Wheee!" yelled the babes.

They traveled fast for a while with the cold spray soaking them and the rush of the river drowning out their attempts to talk. At last, the river took a turn and they drifted into a wider part of the gorge. The river slowed.

Ruffle and Tuffle climbed out of their nests. They mimicked Hemlock's casual pose at the helm of the raft.

"So what are ya' watching for?" Ruffle asked.

Hemlock pointed at a water-soaked tree floating beside them. Then he pointed ahead where the river curved around a bend and disappeared.

"He's watchin' for log jams, course," Tuffle remarked with a know-it-all expression. He crossed his arms and stuck his nose in the air. "We don't wanna' get snagged on one those, right, Hemlock?"

Hemlock hid a smile, and nodded.

Ruffle sneered, and turned his back to the two. "Well, I'll watch for jams *behind* us, then!"

Star popped out of her nest, and sat on the rim of her basket. *Nutty Cappynuts,* she thought. *Thank the moon Hemlock is here.*

Far above the Great Gorge where the nest-raft floated down the Canyon River, a starling with brilliant, fluorescent feathers carried two Twigs on his back – Moon and Feather. Pesky drifted on the currents of air while

Moon searched for his family. The landscape above the rim was only gray ash. He hoped they hid in a cliff cave.

Fern tugged at Moon's arm and pointed down at a speck in the river. They could just make out a bunch of nests clumped together floating along in the middle of the river. Moon yanked Pesky's feathers and shouted at him to fly down to the river. Pesky tilted his head, eyed the clump of nests, and at once spiraled toward it. He reached the raft in a moment, and spread out his wings wide to halt his rapid descent. Peaky hovered just above Star's upturned, surprised face.

"Pesky!" Star screamed in delight. "Moon! Is that you, too, Fern?"

The babes giggled, and tried to grab Pesky's claws, which were tucked into his belly feathers. Irritated, Pesky beat his wings to hover higher.

"Are you all right? Are you safe?" Moon called out to Star.

"Yes! Hemlock saved our lives," Star answered. "We're going to float all the way to the Red Forest, I think. Can you fly ahead and see if the river flows all the way there?"

"Yes, of course," laughed Moon. "It'd be good to know where you're floating to, eh?"

A shadow crossed Star's face. "Fern, what about your family? Are they safe? And Leaf?"

"Mumma and Pappo and the buds are safe," answered Fern. "They are floating west down a fork in the Blue Band. Don't worry about Leaf. He's with Rustle and Feather. They found another way out of the forest. I'm sure he's safe, too."

Abruptly, Pesky whirled over to the river bank and landed on a flat, granite slab. Moon and Fern slid off, and stepped away from the tooler. Pesky scratched at a stone until it turned over. A fat, black beetle raced away, but it was not as quick as Pesky's beak. The tooler stabbed it, swallowed it with a satisfied gulp, and scratched to find another. When it scurried out, Pesky stabbed that one, too, with vicious delight.

Moon exclaimed, "I think Pesky needs to eat again! We better rest here for a while."

The nest-raft spun in circles and floated away. Star waved to Moon. "I guess we'll see you in the Red Forest," she yelled.

"We'll come back and tell you when we see where the river flows," Moon shouted back, and laughed, "If Pesky will let us, that is!" He grinned at Fern. "That will be never, if Pesky doesn't get his belly full here."

From the back of the raft, Ruffle waved to Moon and Fern. He hollered, "Don't worry about us! I'm watching our backs!" With grim determination Ruffle watched the river swirl away behind.

Tuffle sneered at him. "Are you gonna keep watching *behind* us? It's what's *in front* that matters."

Ruffle muttered to himself, "I'd rather look behind me. It's scarier to see what's coming."

Chapter Nineteen

INTO THE DARK

"Well, thank the sun and the moon!" snorted Rustle. "I thought you were melting into the rocks, Leaf!"

After rushing headlong into the dark, the frightened group of Twigs, chipmunks, and marmots now paused to share water and treats. They sat hunched together on the cold rock and listened for scratches from the shadows. The gemstones on the end of their tall walking sticks cast an eerie, bluish radiance on their leafy heads and furry faces.

"Really, Leaf," Feather added. "Why'd you scare us like that? You know your family is safe."

"Uh, sorry," muttered Leaf. *I'm sure Feather is right,* Leaf thought. *Besides, how bad can it be when a bubble bursts on a mountain?*

Feather gave him a worried glance.

"Just look, now. It's not so bad." Rustle pointed at the gemstones. The soft light lit his copper-colored eyes and melted into the shadows. "Our stones stored up the light from the sunlight. They'll help us see in the dark."

"Well, it's not much light, but it is better than none at all," agreed Leaf. "Wonder how long it will last?"

"Another reason to hurry," urged Feather. She tugged Rustle's arm. "Let's get away from here."

Leaf and Rustle stabbed the murky blackness before them with their savers as they marched on with more confident steps. The passageway led them deeper and deeper below the forest, and further from the unsettling tremors. The tunnel's air grew colder, and the Twigs pressed against the chippies for warmth. Fluffles stuffed herself beneath her mum, and peeked from between her front legs.

Whisper pressed her damp nose in Leaf's ear, and *chrrrrrr!'d* a soft chirp to cheer him up.

Every once in a while they stumbled over crumbled pieces of moss where the bottom of the forest had fallen into the tunnel. Hoping to discover a way out, they would circle around, and stare up at a sliver of gray light. But eventually, each time, they decided there was no way to climb the smooth, rounded walls. Each time this happened they grew more and more discouraged. Scrimpy ferns and blossoms clung to the pile of mossy rubble, and offered some nourishment for Fluffles, but not enough for the others.

"It's so cold," murmured Feather as she brushed her fingertips against the curving, black wall. "What is this rock, anyway? I've never seen rocks so black."

"I just want to know where we're all gonna end up," grumbled Rustle. He picked up a sliver of the lava, and whipped it into shadows before them as if he were skipping a rock on water. After a moment the echo bounced back. "There's enough tunnel ahead to walk forever. I bet we're walking under the Sharp Peaks."

"Well, if we are," Feather said at last, "we'd be going west, and will end up in the Red Forest, for sure."

They all grew quiet as they considered this possibility.

"You know something else I've been thinking about?" asked Rustle. "Somethin' made this black rock black. Like maybe it was burned like trees get burnt after a wildfire, you know, Feather? Maybe this rock got so hot somethin' melted it."

Feather glanced at Rustle with huge, anxious eyes. *Could a fire be so hot it would rush through rock and make a tunnel?*

"I've never seen fire that hot," Leaf spoke with a reassuring tone. "Something else made it."

Rustle laughed a nervous laugh. Eager to dispel the glum mood, he continued, "Or... or maybe a giant crawlie lives here! An ugly crawlie with huge teeth that eats rock!" Rustle's voice grew louder as he warmed to his story. "Maybe it's so gigantic it'd crawl right over us and never feel us at all! Or maybe it eats Twigs for treats! Or maybe ..."

"Oh, stop, Rustle," exclaimed Feather with an exasperated tone. "Water probably made this tunnel, that's all, like it digs out rocks behind waterfalls. Anyway, I'm glad it's here. I'm sure this is a shortcut to the Red Forest. This is better than climbing over ridges to get there, don't you think? We're just gonna walk right under them."

Rustle snorted.

All of a sudden, Feather froze with one foot suspended in the air, and her eye wide with alarm. She whispered, "Hush! Something's following us! Something huge!" She whirled around and screamed!

Horrified, Leaf and Rustle gasped and clawed at each other to scramble backwards.

Feather turned around with a smirk on her face, giggling. "Ha! You're not the only one who can make up stories, Rustle."

"That wasn't funny, Feather!" scolded Leaf.

"Pretty good," Rustle chuckled and nodded at Feather with mild admiration.

"AHHHH!" Leaf shrieked, and scattered pebbles as he leapt away. "A bellycrawler!"

From behind a clump of moss, a snake as round and small as Leaf's leg slithered straight toward his toes as if it meant to devour Leaf's foot in one gulp.

"Be still," cried Rustle. "It has no eyes. It's moving toward your shuffling feet, nuthead!

"Forget that!" yelled Leaf as he grabbed Whisper's braid, jumped on her back, and bolted down the tunnel.

Chirping and whistling in alarm Speckles, Claws, Nuzzles, and Fluffles raced after the two. Rustle and Feather trotted after them, laughing. The saver's gemstone bobbed up and down above their heads, shining in the dark.

From behind a rock a nearly sightless, hairless mole squinted to see the glow of Rustle's gemstone bouncing and weaving its way down the tunnel. Then its eyes fixed on the gray bellycrawler slipping away. Sharp claws clicked on the cold rock as it rushed after the helpless, eyeless snake. With a grunt it pounced on the bellycrawler, tore it to pieces, and gobbled it up.

The shriveled mole had become more and more desperate. There were no bulbs and roots hanging down on which it usually feasted. Now starving, it scuttled after the fading laughter of the Twigs. A small snake wasn't much of a meal for a mole. A tiny marmot pup would be more satisfying.

The Twigs chatted and joked as they disappeared in the shadows of the black tube.

But the glow of the gemstone was easy to follow, even for the dull eyes of the digger.

Chapter Twenty

DIGGER ATTACK

Step by step the Twigs, chipmunks, and marmots made their way through the black tube. The chippies curled their bristly tails over their shoulders and gave Feather, Rustle, and Leaf perfect handles to hold. Speckles and Feather led the way followed by the burrowers. Fluffles rode on Nuzzles' back and napped, and for once, Claws kept pace as long as Rustle soothed his nervous twitches. Still, when shadows appeared to leap from the walls, Rustle tugged Claws' ear to keep him from dissolving into a fainting fit. Last, Whisper kept Leaf close beside her.

Leaf felt like he had walked all night. Every so often misty, rainbow-colored fingers of light pierced the crumbling tube's holes above, and trembled on the black rock. The gray cloud which had smothered the forest was gone.

"Nice to see the light again," Feather called back over her shoulder. She patted Speckles' nose and whispered, "You like it, too, don't you, sweetie?"

The chippie trilled a soft *WHRRRR* in response.

With a sharp click, Whisper suddenly jumped sideways.

Leaf screamed, *"AHHH!"* He hopped and twisted around like he was dancing in the dark.

Another gray, stubby snake with no eyes slithered from a shadow, paused a moment, and then squirmed toward Leaf's feet. Against his instincts Leaf froze until the snake crawled away.

Rustle scrunched up his nose, and yanked Claws' ear to keep him calm. "Stop scaring everyone, Leaf. It's only another one of those weird bellycrawlers, Leaf. I can't even tell one end from the other. I can't even see its mouth! I wonder what it eats down here anyway?"

"Muck," growled Leaf.

"Come on, you two," Feather's voice echoed off the walls. "The tunnel isn't getting any shorter."

Leaf squinted at the shadows ahead of them. *Am I imagining that?* A faraway light squeezed sideways through the dark. "Look! Look!" Leaf yelled. He pointed at the distant, twinkling star. "It's the end of the tunnel!"

Rustle grabbed Feather's hand and dragged her down the tunnel. "Come on!"

It seemed to be only an instant later that they stood at the edge of the black tube, bathed in sunlight. Excited and relieved, the scent of trees and fresh air swirled around them. The cave's entrance into the forest was decorated by mud-cloaked strands of hanging ferns. Beyond the tunnel lay purple blossoms and moss covered stones beside a sparkling creek. Bright red elderberries clustered together in lush bushes along well-trodden deer trails.

Unexpectedly, Feather threw up her arms to keep them all from leaping out of the shadows into the forest. "Don't move," she hissed.

Just beyond the entrance, and blocking their path into the woods, a flat-headed badger with a narrow snout dug up the moist earth with its long claws. Dark stripes marked its long hair and ran the length of its body from nose to tail. The badger waddled back and forth as it deepened its future den, only pausing now and then to grub for worms. It was completely oblivious to the Twigs, marmots, and chipmunks, who stood as still as rocks in the shadows of the tunnel watching it dig.

"What's that?" whispered Rustle.

"Yeah, what is it?" whispered Leaf. "It's looks really sweet. I bet it's friendly." He relaxed.

"Wait, Leaf. Don't move. It's a waddler, and they're dangerous even if they look cute," Feather warned them. "I've seen them in the woods across the Wide Valley. It will eat our chippies, and probably go after the burrowers, too. It's making its den right there in front of the tunnel. Even if it goes inside the den, it will be squatting there, and watching for any creature to pass by. We're going to have to jump over it somehow."

Nuzzles and Fluffles shrank further back into the tunnel. The chippies sensed the waddler might attack, so they crouched behind the Twigs.

All at once Nuzzles burst out a piercing whistle. Her fur bristled with alarm, and she pressed Fluffles against the wall. She blasted her alarm again and again. Her eyes gleamed fierce and angry.

With a flurry of scattered dirt the badger disappeared into its den. Only its nose stuck out, ready to defend its burrow.

Whisper gripped Leaf's shoulder strap, and dragged him up onto a ledge. With Fluffles on her back, Nuzzles leapt up behind them. Now she sat bristled up, but quiet.

Speckles bounded up onto the ledge with Feather on his back. Rustle yanked Claws by his tail, and dragged the chippie up. Rustle stood in front of them all. He held his saver across his chest. Leaf and Rustle pointed their gemstones down from the ledge into the shadows. It was enough to see.

The half-starved digger paused just at the edge of the glowing light. Its finger-like pink nose snuffled to locate the scent of the marmot babe. It snorted with anticipation. It claws clicked the rock with an impatient scratching.

Feather slowly pulled her sharpened stone from her belt, and held it ready to slice the mole's squirming nose, if the beast darted toward the ledge.

Nuzzles wore a ferocious expression. She shook Fluffles off her back, and blocked the pup with her body. She was ready to fight to the death.

All at once Rustle snarled like an angry cougar, "*RAASSHHRR!*" which made them all jump.

Leaf slammed his saver on the rocks. *WHACK! WHACK! WHACK!*

The mole hesitated, but its hunger pressed it to crawl closer. Its nose twitched and shivered. Its meal was too close for it to back down.

Leaf spoke low, "I'm going to lead the digger to waddler. Stay here, and protect the burrowers and chippies."

"Leaf, no!" cried Feather.

"No, I'll go!" Rustle insisted.

"You have to stay," Leaf hissed. "They need you more than me." Without another word Leaf dropped from the ledge, and crouched right before the digger.

"Hey, you digger!" Leaf shouted, and poked his saver at the mole's nose. "Want something to eat?" He took a step nearer, and jabbed its nose with the saver. "Come on, then, you ugly beast! Come after me!"

The mole shook his head, and lunged at Leaf, but he jumped backwards, just out of reach. Leaf turned, and sprinted toward badger's den with the mole scurrying after him. At the edge of the tunnel, he stabbed his saver into the ground, and with a beautiful, sailing arc vaulted over the waddler.

Blinded by the sudden, brilliant sunlight, the digger stumbled out of the tunnel, fell, and bounced off the badger's fresh-dug den. It somersaulted just out of reach of the waddler. The badger rushed from its hole. Horrified by the snarling badger, the mole scurried toward the roots of the closest tree, and disappeared.

From a huckleberry thicket just beyond the badger's den, Leaf hurled berries at the badger. "Here," he yelled. "Come get these. Aren't they your favorite?" He tossed the orange berries further and further away from the entrance to the tunnel until, finally, the badger was led into the woods.

"You can come out now," Leaf called to the others. "It's safe!"

Feather was the first to leap from the tunnel. She gave Leaf an enormous hug as she praised him, "Very clever, Leaf, and very brave!"

"I know," replied Leaf with a smug smile. "But I really, really wanted to get out of that black tube. Even a digger and a waddler couldn't stop me now that I can be in the forest again." He took a long, deep breath.

Chapter Twenty-One

ENDLESS WATER

"Just look at this tree!" exclaimed Leaf. He stood beneath the redwood, and studied its bark and lush, deep green fronds. Leaf looked up, but the tree grew so tall he could not see its tip. So many sunbursts sparkled through its limbs it was as if hundreds of stars perched in them. The redwood's branches stretched out like they wished to embrace the cool mist. *These old trees grow as tall as the Old Seeder,* Leaf realized with astonishment. *There are other trees here just as tall...even taller!*

"It's the Red Forest!" Feather whispered, awestruck. "We're here."

"Whoaaa!" Rustle whooped. "If there are giant trees that means there are giant leaves here that will be perfect for leaf-flyers!"

Delighted to be free of the gloom of the tunnel Claws somersaulted into a patch of moss and mushrooms.

Stuck upside-down, pieces of golden mushrooms decorated his belly. Speckles and Whisper pulled him out. Nuzzles and Fluffles shuffled from one stand of blue flowers to another, and ate as many blossoms as they could stuff in their cheeks.

Leaf glanced back at the snaking, dark tube. *Will I ever return to the South Forest?* he wondered.

Rustle slapped Leaf's shoulder. "Come on, Leaf. Let's climb a tree. Let's find out what's up there." He leaned back, and pointed up. "Come on!" Rustle grabbed Leaf's arm, and yanked him to one of the massive trunks.

Feather interrupted, "No, no, we have to find the others first." She looked back and forth through the trees. "This forest seems endless! Which way should we go? How will we find them?"

"Does the Blue Band even flow all the way to the Red Forest?" worried Leaf.

Rustle pointed at the creek, and then to the west. "Look. It's flowing downhill. This stream will end up wherever the Blue Band flows. So, that's the way to go."

"I think Rustle's right," agreed Feather.

Rustle took a step, and then paused. "Hey, do you hear that funny noise? Listen. It's sort of like wind blowing, but it's not wind."

A gentle, rhythmic *RUSH, RUSH, RUSH* filled the air. Salt lingered in the mist.

"Do you taste that?" Feather smacked her lips. "Strange. It's like the white rock the soft-eyes lick in the caves. And just smell this air." She wrinkled up her nose in distaste.

"Kinda' smells like rotten, wet grass." Rustle held his nose. "Whatever it is, it's slimy, for sure."

"Well it's coming from the west and that's the way we have to go," declared Leaf. "Let's go."

They followed the creek. The *RUSH, RUSH, RUSH* grew closer and the odd smell became overpowering.

"Look at that!" exclaimed Leaf as he took a step from the mossy creek bank onto a band of sparkling, smooth sand.

The sand bordered a boundless expanse of water heaving up and down beneath a shimmering mist. The tips of the ocean's waves curled over, rushed toward Leaf with a foaming trim, and then rushed back out, away from his toes. The waves floated gently from the shore like foamy decorations trailing silver ribbons.

"It's the Endless Water," Leaf said, awestruck. "It's just like the stories PapaMook told us."

Feather and Rustle blinked at Leaf with questioning eyes.

"One time long ago PapaMook wandered to the end of the West Forest," Leaf explained. "He found the Endless Water, but he didn't like it at all because there weren't any more trees." Leaf threw out his arms as if to embrace the ocean. Exhilarated by the thrumming waves and salty spray, he yelled, "We're here! The Endless Water!"

"Makes sense," stated Feather matter-of-factly. "A forest has to stop somewhere, I guess."

Speckles didn't care much for the open sky above him, so he chirped a warning to Claws and Whisper to remain in the protective cover of the trees. Nuzzles and Fluffles squeezed into the hollow of a bleached piece of driftwood, and promptly fell asleep.

Feather glanced at the chippies and burrowers. "Yes, you better stay there for now."

Just then seagulls screamed overhead. Pink crabs on the beach hastened to bury themselves in the sand.

Leaf ducked and covered his head.

Rustle grabbed him and Feather, and dragged them under a clump of slimy sea grass. "Try not to get eaten by skyhunters on our first day here, eh?" he exclaimed.

Still, they were all fascinated, by the pink crabs and seagulls. They peeked out of the grass, and watched a seagull attack a crab.

"Phew, Rustle!" protested Feather. "You could have picked a better place to stuff us!" She popped out, and washed off the stink in the clear water of the creek. "Here, Rustle. Get in here. You need a wash, too. And so do you, Leaf!" she giggled and splashed water on Leaf and Rustle.

After a complete soaking, Leaf sat on the driftwood above the hollow where the marmots slept. His gaze followed the beach to the north and then to the south. *Where did the Blue Band bring my family?* he wondered. *North or south?*

Rustle and Feather joined him on the log. They sat listening to the screams of the greedy seagulls.

All of a sudden Leaf leapt atop the log. "Listen! Do you hear that? It sounds like..."

Mixed in with the screams of the seagulls it sounded as if two Twig babes were shrieking with delight. Not far from where Leaf stood on top of the driftwood, Pappo and Mumma lifted Buddy and Burba from their basket-raft, and set them loose on the beach. The slippers had pulled them all the way to the Endless Water.

"Is it...?" Feather gasped.

"It is!" laughed Rustle.

Leaf beamed. "It's the buds!"

Chapter Twenty-Two

SNAPPERS

Hemlock stood on the rim of his nest at the front of the raft, and watched the river flowing away from him. Moon and Fern had not come back to tell them where they were headed. Next to him Tuffle had propped himself up on his elbows. He looked more as if he were napping than helping Hemlock keep watch. Hemlock's rope had held the nest-raft together secure and tight all through the night. Except for Star and him, all the Twigs had fallen asleep. Hemlock glanced back at Star.

Star was perched on the rim of the last nest, which floated next to Ruffle's. He had slipped down in his as if it were a cradle. The tips of his feathers blew up and down to match his snoring. Star watched a crimson sunrise glimmer behind them. It set the fog aglow, which smothered the water. Star had felt suffocated by the fog, but once the pink rays of the sun pierced it she felt better.

The raft floated over a submerged log, stuck there for a moment, and then pulled itself free. The river splashed the side of the raft as it rocked back and forth, soothing all who still slept. A fish jumped to catch a long-legged fly on the surface of the water, and splashed Ruffle. The next instant, the fish and the fly were gone.

Ruffle poked his head up from his nest with an abrupt jerk. He blinked and yawned. Star watched him with an amused grin, and so at once he sat up rigid in a guard-like pose. He stared at the river flowing away behind them with a serious expression.

Star patted his head. "It's just a little splashing, Ruffle. Don't worry."

From the front of the raft Tuffle roused himself, and called back to his brother, "How's the river flowing back there, Ruffle? Creeping up on us, is it, eh?" He snorted, and chuckled.

With a glum expression Ruffle shrugged, and turned away from Star. He studied the ripples behind the raft, and hoped his cheeks were not glowing too pink.

Star suppressed a giggle. She climbed over the babes, who yawned and grumbled for breakfast. Without delay Star handed out morning treats to the Twig babes, PapaMook, Sapper, the Cappynut twins, and Hemlock.

The sticktytoes and looksalots stared at the water. Darting dragonflies and slender longlegs danced between morning sunbursts, and sparkled on the river. Long, pink tongues uncurled and whipped out to catch their unsuspecting prey one after the other. Soon Click, Chirp, Crunch, Veil, and Sky enjoyed full bellies.

Now the river flowed wide, shallow, and flat like the gray clouds it reflected. Bubbles popped on the surface where odd creatures with pinching claws hid beneath the muddy shore. Sun-bleached trunks of long-dead trees lay half-submerged in the shallow water. After a while the river emptied into a wide marsh full of smelly muck.

With slow swirls the river continued west. Steep bluffs rose up on either side. Atop the great bluffs towered enormous redwood trees with cinnamon-colored bark and thin, fern-like needles. In the swollen heart of each tree spiraled the colors of the same crimson sunrise which greeted Star. The wandering roots of the redwoods intertwined with others. Their branches embraced the drifting mist, and their tips tickled the fading stars.

The sound of an unfamiliar pounding of faraway waves gave the babes a reason to balance on the rims of their nests. They stretched on tip-toe to see. "What is it, PapaMook?" they asked in unison.

"It's the Endless Water," PapaMook explained. "I saw it once long ago." He spoke low as if he were sharing a horrible, terrifying secret, "There are no trees there!"

"Oooh," cried the Twig babes.

Soon the Endless Water came into view. All were mesmerized. Foaming waves scattered shells on the sand like Twigs tossing pebbles on the Old Seeder's floor. Enormous, bleached logs lay intertwined on the shore. The babes looked at each other – delighted. It was a perfect place to play hide-and-seek. Star-shaped creatures floated in the shallow tide pools, beckoning the babes to float on them. The sky was shrouded with the gray mist.

Hemlock nodded to Star and pointed to the mucky shoreline. By his grim expression Star could tell he did not like being out in the open like this.

He wants to hide in the grass on the riverbank. Star glanced at the huge, white flyers diving to spear creatures on the beach. The seagulls fought over the crabs and ripped them to shreds. *We should do as Hemlock says.* "All right, babes," Star called out. "We need to hide in the grass over there. Let's try to make our nest float that way."

Hemlock grabbed soaked leaves, which stuck out on limbs from half-drowned trees, and used them to pull the raft closer to the bank. The Twig babes rocked their nests back and forth, and reached for slime-coated strips of grass. In this way they all pulled the nest-raft along from sticks to grass and sticks again. At last the riverbank drew near.

All of sudden, a squeaky voice cried out from the rear of the raft. "There! Look there!" Ruffle screamed. "Hide! Everybody hide!" He grabbed Pool, who was the nearest Twig babe to him, and yanked him down beneath the rim of the nest.

Stunned at Ruffle's cry, the others stared in disbelief, wondering whether they should laugh or shout at Ruffle's silliness.

Then Tuffle snorted. "Look at him. What a nuthead. He just wants attention." Tuffle sneered louder, "Did you finally spot something creeping up behind us, then, eh?"

The babes giggled, "Ruffle's a nuthead! Ruffle's a nuthead!"

Hemlock and Star exchanged curious looks. PapaMook scratched his head. With creaking knees he tried to balance in his nest, and see what had frightened Ruffle so much.

Only Sapper knew Ruffle's cry was real. "Everyone quiet!" he ordered. "Be still. And it's best if you go ahead and hide for now." He crawled over the heads of the babes. Tuffle followed, smashing the heads of the babes who did not duck down in their nest quick enough.

Ruffle and Pool peeked at the water swirling behind the raft. Intent, and half-afraid, they stared at the ripples. A green, flat nose with a hooked mouth swam toward the nest-raft. Eyes like glistening beads fixed on the stickytoes and looksalots. The river turtle had found its breakfast.

"Ruffle! Tuffle! Quick!" shouted Sapper. "Your slingers!" He ripped his slingshot from his belt, snatched a dragonfly, which had just alighted on the raft, loaded it into his slinger, aimed, and shot it at the turtle. The dragonfly bounced off the turtle's scaly nose.

At once the Cappynut twins leapt onto the rims of the nests, and reached for nearby longlegs skimming the surface of the water. Ruffle and Tuffle snatched dragonflies and water bugs from the air and water, and loaded their slingshots. Bugs whizzed right and left of the turtle. Surprised, the turtle realized its breakfast was flying directly at him. It stopped paddling toward the raft, and drifted with the currents. The flies continued to come whooshing and bouncing off its head.

"That should keep it busy for a while," declared Sapper, "but we better get out of the water."

"Hurry, Hemlock," cried Star, "we need to reach the grass and hide! Come babes. Come help."

The looksalots and stickytoes were terrified by the turtle. They flung out their tongues, and grasped one mucky limb after another to pull the raft even closer to the embankment. They soon reached the shore, and the frightened stickytoes and looksalots were the first to crawl into the grass.

Star watched Veil and Sky scramble up the bank. "I've never seen a looksalot move so fast," she remarked to Hemlock with a grin. "Hurry now, all of you, into the grass. We must hurry to the giant trees up there!" She pointed to the top of the bluff.

Tuffle and Ruffle leapt from the nests to the shore. They continued to slingshot dragonflies and longlegs at the turtle, although it had now lost all interest in chasing the raft.

Tuffle threw an arm around Ruffle. "Guess you were right, brother. It is a good idea to keep an eye on what's behind you. You never know what might creep up!" He shoved his brother ahead into the thick grass.

A sheepish grin spread over Ruffle's face. He didn't often get a compliment from Tuffle. He glanced over his shoulder. "Yeah. Gotta' look behind you... and in front of you, too, I guess. Only I don't see anything in front of us, do you?"

The Cappynuts came to an abrupt stop. "Where'd they all go?" whispered Tuffle. The tall grass stood dense and still in front of their noses.

Behind them Hemlock wrapped his rope over his shoulder. He hopped off the raft, brushed past the Cappynut twins with a puzzled glance, and disappeared into the grass.

Star called from somewhere in the thick stalks ahead of them, "Hurry up, you two. We don't want to lose you now." She popped out of the grass and pushed the twins in front of her. "Hurry up!"

The Cappynuts stumbled over each other. "All right, all right," they grumbled. "We were just checking behind us."

"We must hurry," Star urged them. "We're almost there." *Leaf will be looking for us.*

CHAPTER TWENTY-THREE

BEACHED TWIGS

With sharpened twigs Buddy and Burba popped the glistening bubbles gurgling up in the sand.

"What's down dere?" wondered Buddy.

"Beasts," declared Burba. "Bubble beasts."

Mumma stood on the beach with an upturned chin, and gazed at the gigantic trees in the forests behind them. Then she turned to stare at the silver waves splashing on the shore blanketed by thick, creeping fog. "Are we here?" she asked Pappo. "The Red Forest, I mean. Are we here?" Mumma's voice was full of wonder. The strange splash of endless waves and the salty smell overwhelmed her.

They had slept on the raft all through the night while the slippers pulled them west. They drifted past a meadow where the splintering noise of falling trees woke Pappo. An enormous silhouette of a goliath beaver crouched on a log, and watched the raft pass. Pappo had waved, and Slapper had waved back.

As dawn broke they were left stranded where the river spilled into the shallow pools of a beach. The sand sprawled out from the toes of the redwoods.

The slippers slipped free of their ropes, and joined a family of playful otters sliding down a muddy embankment.

Mumma waved to the river otters, and called out, "Thank you! Fare well, friends!"

"So yeah, is dis it den? Da Red Forest?" Buddy asked. "Whoa!" A pink claw appeared in the sand beside a bubble he had just popped.

Burba whacked the claw, and then stated matter-of-factly, "This isn't the Red Forest, nuthead. It's green and brown. We're in the green forest."

"Oh, dat's right," agreed Buddy. He whacked the claw, too, and nodded his head with a solemn expression. "Dere's a brown forest, too, don't ya' dink? And maybe a blue one."

Pappo swept his arm in an arc toward the giant trees. "Yes, this is the Red Forest. We're here." He frowned at the twins. "Stop bothering the creatures here. You don't know what they might do. They may not like Twigs. I'm sure they don't like to be whacked," Pappo warned the twins with an ominous tone in his voice.

"*WHOAAAA!*" shrieked Burba.

"Watch out!" Mumma screamed.

The pink claw poking from the sand was joined by another. With furious clicks and whirls they pinched the air. Behind the claws, a pink-shelled body popped out of the sand. Two antennae whirled above angry, black eyes, and flashed at Burba. Then the crab rose up on its stick-like legs, and scuttled into the water.

"Look at it go!" shouted the twins.

AAAAAKKKKKK! AAAAAAKKKKKK! The unexpected screams of the giant white seagulls stunned the Twigs.

Pappo's voice bellowed out, "Fall over! Lie flat and pretend to be sticks!" At once all of the Twigs flattened themselves on the sand. The gulls lost interest and drifted away. Once the gulls left, Pappo ordered, "Into the woods now and stay hidden in the roots. Let's not be foolish and stand around in the open until we know this land well."

"And den we can be foolish?" asked Buddy.

Pappo's face softened. "Yes, Buddy. Then we can do lots of foolish things. But not right now. Come back to the trees." Pappo stood in the roots of a redwood, leaned back, and tried to see its tip. "These trees are as tall as those in the South Forest. Actually, they seem taller," he remarked.

Just then a frenzy of whacks brought a shower of needles down on Pappo. *FLAPPP, FLAPPP, WHACCKK, FLAPPP!* Two out-of-control wings slid through the limbs above the Twigs.

"A skyhunter!" screamed Mumma. Panicked, she piled moss on top of Buddy and Burba.

Just then Pesky plopped from the sky onto a clump of moss near Mumma. His wings were stuck together by sap-covered needles. Angry, he plucked needles from his feathers, and then had to claw them off his beak. Of course, they then stuck to his claws, so he hopped around in the sand, trying to scratch them off.

Fern and Moon slid off his back. Moon calmed the tooler with a pat on his neck, and helped pull the sappy needles off his claws.

"Mumma, it's me!" Fern shouted to the ball of moss shivering in the roots.

Moon yelled over his shoulder, "And me too. And Pesky. Sorry for the scare."

Fern dug the twins from under the moss and hugged them tight. Mumma and Pappo threw their arms around them all in a Twig-ball embrace.

"Well, of course, it's you!" Pappo stated matter-of-factly with a nod of his head. "Thank the sun and moon, you're safe."

"Yes, and thank Moon, too!" laughed Fern.

Mumma cried, "Oh, I'm so happy to see you!"

Burba and Buddy tried to hug Pesky but the tooler hopped away from the trees and onto the beach in a huff. The bubbles in the sand caught his eye. He hopped around in circles, and stabbed at them with his sharp beak.

"Watch out, Pesky! Dose are bubble beasts!" Buddy warned him.

"Shhhh!" Burba whispered. "I wanna' see what happens."

Pesky stabbed at the twitching sand. It wasn't long before pink claws appeared, clicking and pinching at whatever was near. It happened to be Pesky's beak. They caught hold of his beak, and in a frantic frenzied toss Pesky hurled the crab into the air. *AAAAWWWWKKKK!* he screamed.

The twins squealed with delight.

"Be still! Listen!" Pappo exclaimed. "Shhh! Quiet down. Listen!"

From far up the beach, which was lost in the fog, a voice shouted, "Pappo! Pappo! We're here!"

Mumma rushed out into the fog, followed by the others. A slender figure with emerald green, leafy hair sprinted down the beach toward them.

Leaf waved frantically. "Mumma!"

Buddy and Burba raced toward Leaf, and tackled him in the sand. Laughing with joy, he freed himself, and stumbled into the arms of Pappo and Mumma. Fern leapt on the huddle with her own cries of delight. Moon grinned from ear to ear.

Rustle and Feather hung back, waiting for the Old Seeder Twigs to notice they were there, too.

As soon as Leaf appeared from within the huddle Moon grasped Leaf's hand, and cried, "Great to see you, good friend!"

"Moon!" exclaimed Leaf. "Is Star here, too?" He looked past Moon, searching for Star. "Did you fly here on Pesky, then?" With sudden concern, he glanced up at the sky in case Pesky came crashing down on him.

"He's over there," Moon reassured him, and pointed down the beach where Pesky was busy stabbing more bubbles in the sand. "I see you all made it safely," he added, motioning to the chippies, Rustle, and Feather.

"Oh, Leaf, burrowers came with you," whispered Fern. "A tiny one, too. How sweet!" She tiptoed over to watch Fluffles and Nuzzles eat some purple blossoms. Whisper, Speckles, and Claws joined them.

"Is Star here?" Leaf asked again.

"They were still floating down the Canyon River last time I saw them," answered Moon. "I'm sure they made it to the Endless Water, though. The river spills out somewhere up there." He pointed to the north. "I flew back to tell them where their river ended, but these huge, white skyhunters chased us away." He nodded at the seagulls who were circling above.

"Come back to the trees," cautioned Pappo. This is no place for Twigs to wander."

"No. We need to go find them," urged Leaf. "Look! A mist is covering the water. The white skyhunters are leaving. They can't fly in this thick mist. Look!" He pointed at the fog curling around the lower branches of the redwoods. "The trees are disappearing. We can go now! Let's go!"

"Shhh!" Moon waved for everyone to be silent. He was staring up the beach. The fog bank could not quite completely smother a gentle laugh mixed with teeny giggles.

"Star!" Leaf yelled. He bolted up the beach at once, and disappeared in the swirling mist.

"Leaf!" a muffled voice called back to him.

Star must have been running toward Leaf because somewhere in the fog, out of sight of the others, Star and Leaf found each other, and embraced.

Chapter Twenty-Four

THE RED FOREST

All were finally together, drifting in and out of the fog sharing hugs and greetings.

"Look at all dose Twig babes," whispered Buddy. He nudged Burba, and pointed at Breeze, Cone, Mist, Sand, and Moss. Pool stood in front of the babes as if on guard against Buddy and Burba. Pool wondered if he was older than the Old Seeder buds, and if he could boss them around, too.

The Twig babes blew spit-bubbles, and giggled.

"Why are dey doing dat?" Buddy asked Pool.

"Because they're still babes," he replied.

"Allo dere," murmured Buddy with a shy smile. They pushed past Pool at once, crowded around Buddy, and giggled. "Wanna' go look for dings? Bet dere's some dings over dere."

"Yes, let's go look for dings!" cried the babes. "Let's go look for dings!"

Buddy led the babes over to a sea kelp pile. They poked sticks at it to see if crabs might scuttle out and pinch their toes.

"Why don't you go play with the buds?" Pool told Burba. "Buds should stick together."

"You're not any older than they are," sneered Burba. "Bet I'm older than you."

"Are not," disagreed Pool.

"Are too," retorted Burba.

Hemlock walked out of the fog. He stood beside Pool, and placed his hand on the young sprout's shoulder. With a solemn face he studied Burba.

Not knowing whether to be awestruck or worried, Burba asked, "Who are you?"

"He doesn't talk, so don't bother him," Pool answered in a stern voice. "We call him Hemlock."

Leaf popped from the fog, and gave Pool a sideways glance. "I'm sure Burba won't bother him, Pool. I want you *both* to respect his ways. Star told me Hemlock's very brave. Maybe one day he'll teach you his ways. Maybe even show you how to make an amazing rope like his."

Hemlock grinned and walked away. Pool and Burba tagged along behind, and pestered him with questions, which Hemlock shrugged off.

Fern and Moon wandered away from the others. As they walked near a bleached-white piece of driftwood an odd whimper caught their attention. A clump of sea grass squiggled and twisted.

"Oh, a creature is stuck in there," Fern cried.

"Wonder what?" Moon stuck it with a stick.

Eeerrkk! Eeerrkkk!

"Stop it, Moon!" protested Fern.

Eeerrkk! Eeerrkkk! Eeerrkk! Eeerrkkk! The creature whimpered for help.

Fern reached out to the mass of sea kelp.

"Be careful," Moon whispered. He held Fern's arm back. "The creatures of the Red Forest are different from what we know."

Fern paused, considered Moon's warning, and then shook off his hold. With a gentle hand she lifted a strand of kelp.

At once the odd mewing stopped and the pile became still.

Fern continued to lift one strand after another. "Oh, Moon, look," Fern chuckled. "It's a babe!"

At the sound of her voice the mewing began again. *Eeerrkk! Eeerrkkk!*

Fern peeled back the strands until a wet, black nose surrounded by shivering whiskers appeared. The nose twitched. A tiny, pursed mouth blew bubbles, and the bubbles popped with each breath it took. Two round, moist eyes blinked at Fern. The sea otter pup whimpered. *Eeerrkk! Eeerrkkk!*

Fern giggled. "What *are* you? A lost babe, eh? Where's your mum? Did we scare her away?"

Moon cautioned Fern, "Her mum may be close by. She won't like us so close to her babe even if you are trying to help it." Worried, he scanned the beach and water for the mum. Not far offshore a dark head bobbed up and down between curling waves. "I think that's her mum right out there, Fern. Hurry, before she comes after us!"

"I don't think her mum has ever seen Twigs before, Moon, or she'd already be ripping us to splinters! She must be afraid of us, poor thing." Fern patted the pup's muzzle, and kissed it before she released the squirming the seal pup from the last strand of kelp.

The pup sat up, shook its tiny body, nuzzled Fern's face, and then blew a rainbow-colored bubble in her hair.

"I think I'll call you Fuzzy!" laughed Fern.

With an abrupt burst of awkwardness, the pup waddled to the water, and dove beneath the waves. Right away her mum swam to her, and nuzzled her babe all over. Then the mum rolled over on her back. Fuzzy climbed on her belly, and the two floated up and down on the waves. The mum stared at Fern and Moon with a curious expression. She seemed to be wondering *what kind of creatures are these who freed her babe?*

Fern waved to the mum and pup. "Bye, friends! Hope I see you again!"

Moon murmured, "Good job, Fern."

Fern turned to Moon with glowing eyes. "I love the Red Forest. There must be many creatures here we've never ever seen before. How wonderful it's going to be to discover them all."

"Sure," Moon agreed. "And maybe there are other Twigs here, too."

"You think so?" Fern wondered. She looked around with an expectant expression. "Maybe there are and they are watching us right now!" Not seeing any, she returned to studying the sea otters. They were cracking shells together and gobbling up whatever was inside.

Not far away, behind a bleached piece of driftwood, Twigs with long pine needles for hair, shimmering blue eyes, and sap-sticky fingers whispered to each other as they spied on the new Twigs who had arrived in the Red Forest.

A sudden sadness softened Fern's voice. "Moon, do you think we might lose the Red Forest like we lost the Old Seeder?"

Moon glanced over his shoulder at the towering trees lining the bluff behind them. "Well, we'll never know for sure what might happen." He picked up a slimy strand of sea weed and waved it around. "But I do know we will take good care of what we have in front of our noses," he chuckled. His voice grew soft as he gazed into Fern's eyes. "We're going to love what we have in front of us a lot more, too, now that we nearly lost everything."

Pesky hopped past the two Twigs. Fern and Moon grinned at each other as the silly tooler eyed a bubble twinkling on the sand above a buried crab. Pesky pranced around the bubble, and then furiously stabbed at it with his beak. With angry jerks he tilted his head back forth as another bubble blew up between his claws.

The sea otters dared to float closer to the Twigs. They rolled around on the beach in the foaming waves, and kept a wary eye on Pesky, who glared at them and continued to stab bubbles.

Fern whispered as if making a promise to the sea otters, "I will live here in this beautiful place, and learn all about you. Maybe one day, you will trust me, and we will play together. This is my home now. It's where I want to stay." She looked at Moon, a question in her eyes.

Moon smiled and nodded. "Then I will stay here, too. Just to be with Pesky, of course."

Fern laughed.

*When a volcano erupts, small mammals
hide deep in the earth and survive.
As time goes by trees sprout and plants grow.
Beavers, birds, elk, and more animals return.
New ecosystems replace the old.
Adapting to change is what creatures do.
Will you change with our climate, too?*

Watch Over Wildlife

Hoary Marmot

What are they called?
Marmots
Where do they live?
Washington Cascades
Why are they endangered?

Some marmot populations may have decreased by half in the past 25 years. One of the prime suspects is climate change. Snowpack, lack of water resources, and reduced alpine vegetation are impacted and lost due to drought. Hibernation is interrupted by earlier, warmer seasons, yet food sources are not as plentiful. Marmots are also increasingly vulnerable to new predators like coyotes which are continually seeking new habitats in which to breed and survive. Recent studies suggest the marmots may recover within protected geographic pockets.

Watch Over Wildlife

Sea Otter

What are they called?
Sea Otter
Where do they live?
Pacific Northwest coasts
Why are they endangered?

Sea otters are a keystone species and are often called "global warming warriors". They keep sea urchins in check so kelp forests can thrive. Kelp ecosystems offer shelter for other species and reduce greenhouse gases. Otters are threatened by loss of habitat, marine pollution, disease, and fishing nets. They are increasingly threatened by predators like killer whales whose habitats are also impacted by climate change. Recent conservation efforts have helped increase sea otter populations.

Watch Over Wildlife

Townsend's Big-Eared Bats

What are they called?
Big-eared Bats
Where do they live?
Caves, dense forests, protected habitats
Why are they endangered?

The population of big-eared bats in the Pacific Northwest has decreased nearly 80% in the last thirty years. Bats eat thousands of insects each day and keep ecosystems in balance, but pesticide use destroys their food supply. Climate change alters their roosting, foraging, and drinking resources due to drought and below-freezing temperatures. Their decline is mostly due to cave exploration, logging, and colony disturbance. Conservationists are working to provide safe breeding habitats.

Watch Over Wildlife

Salamanders

What are they called?
Long-toed Salamanders
Where do they live?
Forests, ponds, lakes, streams, and wetlands
Why are they endangered?

Salamander populations are on the decline. Drought due to climate change is drying wetland areas where salamanders breed and survive. Aquatic plants are impacted, too. Salamanders are hatching before there is enough food to survive. Also, clear-cut forests and foreign species like trout and fungus are impacting salamanders. Recent relocation and adaption action plans by conservationists are helping to increase their chances for survival.

ABOUT THE AUTHOR
JO MARSHALL

JO MARSHALL lives in the Pacific Northwest near glacier-capped volcanoes and lush rainforests. She is concerned about climate change impacting the wildlife and forests in this region, and so her timely novels describe this transforming natural world with stories of fantastic adventures about impish and courageous stick creatures called Twigs.

Jo volunteered as a literacy tutor for elementary school children in Snohomish, Washington for seven years. In the D.C. area from 1999 to 2006 she worked for the Paralyzed Veterans of America and Oceana as a legal assistant to their General Counsels. Jo earned a B.A. in German Language and Literature from the University of Maryland, Europe in 1986. From 1984-1987 she worked as a liaison between the military and international communities in West Berlin.

Jo contributes to, promotes, and is a member of many conservation nonprofits.

ABOUT THE ARTIST
D.W. MURRAY

D.W. MURRAY is an award-winning Disney and Universal Pictures artist, whose screen credits include *Mulan, Tarzan, Lilo & Stitch, Brother Bear, Curious George,* and many more. An award recipient of the prestigious New York Society of Illustrators Gallery, his talent is recognized by the 2004 Gold Aurora Award. He wrote numerous screenplays, pitched story concepts to Roy Disney, and to the producers of *Touched By An Angel.* He is a former scriptwriter for *Big Ideas* and the colorful children's animated series *3-2-1 Penguins.*

D.W. Murray is the author of the thrilling fantasy novels *Majesty -The Sorcerer and the Saint,* and *Majesty and the Dragon's Throne,* which are compared to the Chronicles of Narnia. Find out more about D.W. Murray on his website, www.dwmurraybooks.com.

More Twig Stories by Jo Marshall

Leaf & the Rushing Waters

Leaf & the Sky of Fire

Leaf & the Long Ice

www.twigstories.com

Leaf & the Rushing Waters

A glacier lake bursts its ice dam, and Leaf's ancient tree home is flooded, his family trapped, and rescue is far away across dangerous grasslands. With the help of jittery chipmunks and brave Twig friends, a determined Leaf sets off on a desperate quest for help – to find a goliath beaver!

Leaf & the Sky of Fire

In a dying forest, infested with bark beetles, Twigs are trapped by barkbiters, and forced to hide in a cave. Salamanders and a misplaced chameleon are their loyal guards. Leaf attempts a foolhardy rescue, but now the Twigs and their friends are in greater peril – chased by barkbiters and a firestorm!

Leaf & the Long Ice

Enticed by stories of vanishing snow and rare beasts, Leaf's twin brothers, Buddy and Burba, hitch a ride on a giant moth to the shrinking glacier of Echo Peak. But when they are lost in a maze of ice tunnels Leaf, a weird hermit, and the rare beasts of the ice are their only hope for rescue!

www.twigstories.com

Made in the USA
Middletown, DE
21 March 2016